OUR COLONY BEYOND THE CITY OF RUINS

OUR COLONY BEYOND THE CITY OF RUINS

JANALYN GUO

SUBITO PRESS 2018

ISBN: 978-0-9988594-5-3

Cover design & typesetting by HR Hegnauer
    www.hrhegnauer.com
Original cover images available in the creative commons include
    photographs by Xia Aike and Miltos Gikas as well as from the
    Library of Congress archive
Text typeset in Adobe Garamond Pro and Futuremoon

Subito Press
Department of English
University of Colorado at Boulder
226 UCB
Boulder, CO 80309-0226
subitopress.org

Distributed by Small Press Distribution
1341 Seventh Street
Berkeley, California 94710
spdbooks.org

Generous funding for this publication has been provided by the Creative
Writing Program in the Department of English and the Innovative Seed
Grant Program at the University of Colorado at Boulder.

CONTENTS

BLOOM

My aunt owned a small gua sha parlor in Fushun, China. It was a converted storage space, squeezed tightly between an arcade and a bathhouse. If you held your ear up against one wall, you could hear the plinky electronic music coming out of the gaming cabinets. If you held your ear up to the other wall, you could hear water gurgling through pipes and the shouting of men in the midst of their bathhouse conversations. My aunt slapped a red paisley patterned paper on the walls and decorated the space with a few animal figurines, vases full of long peacock feathers, and some candles. Soft music played in the background. Only six cots fit inside the room, almost touching at the corners.

My aunt's customers were mainly men who enjoyed traditional cures. Lying shirtless on their bellies, they explained their ailments to her as she poured a homemade ointment onto their bare backs and rubbed it into their skin. She scraped at specific places on their backs with a wooden tool until red sand-like blotches appeared. Pointing at the red zones, she explained to her customers what they meant—weak lungs, weak heart, excess fire or wind. Their bodies glistened with perspiration and released heat into the room.

I handed my aunt glass cups, one by one, for the cupping process, which she performed immediately following gua sha to help the blood flow. The cups came in a variety of sizes, to fit the many parts of the back. My aunt swirled a piece of flaming cotton around in each cup before quickly sticking it onto a body. I watched the skin rise into each cup, muffin-like, and turn purplish in color. Sucked up into a multitude of glass orbs, parts of the back would grow so taut that pores that had once been invisible darkened into black holes as they stretched open. This was when we let the skin breathe for some time.

My aunt performed the final steps with a cold precision. She twisted the cups off one by one and studied the shade of the purple welts. She told her customers to refrain from bathing for a few days because their pores were wide open and vulnerable. They looked at their lumpy discolored backs in the mirror before walking out the door.

. . .

It was the start of my twenty-fifth spring, and I was staying with my aunt after a year of bad luck. I had lost my job, ended things with my first serious boyfriend, and required major surgery to remove a tumor from my body, which turned out to be benign. My parents suggested I spend some time in China, to cleanse my spirit. My aunt agreed to take me in.

"Well, it was your zodiac year," my aunt said, when I told her about my woes. "I bet you didn't bother to wear red." People in China took their zodiac years seriously. It happened once every twelve years of your life, when your zodiac sign repeated itself. I was a tiger, and my zodiac year had just come to a close. According to my aunt, wearing red could have driven away some of the bad luck.

I liked the routine of the parlor. We opened up at nine and locked up at four. In the last moments of sunlight, we walked down the busy streets and around the reservoir, which was lined with trees whose trunks were painted white with medicine. On the way to and from the apartment, there was a farmer's market where vendors clustered together with their goods. I liked the complicated smell of their presence, the foul odors of seafood and raw meats laid out in pails and along truck beds tangled with the smells of freshly made noodles and scallion pancakes. Every Sunday, we bought three kilos of hazelnuts.

An abundance of motes, spores, and seedpods rained down on us that spring. They hung lazily in the air, traveled with the wind, and clung to my hair and the collar of my coats. On our walks, my aunt complained about her customers: this one a wife beater, that one a hotheaded drunk, and a quiet one that gambled away his family's prized car. She wished that her procedures could suck those bad qualities out. Then she looked out at the landscape and smiled. She told me about a small batch of customers she had every spring whose pores opened up especially big. She called them "men in bloom." They returned to the parlor, angry and fearful, to show her that their backs were sprouting flowers or vegetables or baby trees. My aunt took them into a private room where she assured them that there was nothing to worry about. She sat them down and asked them: Well, isn't this what you wanted, to be changed? She taught them how to tend their new growths with tiny shears. My aunt had a soft spot for these men.

It turned out that there would be an abundance of men in bloom that spring when I was in town. I met many of them in person. They grew close to my aunt and walked around the reservoir with us. I walked arm-in-arm with a customer who grew peonies, another who grew pears, another who grew a very thin bamboo forest, and another who grew water lilies. ("He is like a great pond," my aunt told me, "very weepy when we are alone.") Their backs grew wide and wild. They explained to me that a patch of nature living on their backs, though burdensome, provided a number of benefits. It cleaned the blood. It increased the availability of oxygen. Their feelings of pain were lifted. They felt softened.

Among the men in bloom that spring, my aunt fell for a man named Walt Suo.

. . .

One night, my aunt invited Walt Suo over for dinner. Before his arrival, we tidied up. My aunt's apartment was small but cozy. It was full of plants. She had a fondness for succulents. Their fat stalks cluttered the windowsills, spines everywhere. She liked the rarity of their bloom, and her framed photographs of their flowers over the years hung on the walls of each room.

Walt wore a flat cap, an oversized leather jacket, and dress pants. When he took off his cap, I saw that he had once been bald but was now growing a lush patch of mushrooms where his hair had been. My aunt dropped a bag of hazelnuts on the coffee table and gave us a hammer to keep us busy while dinner simmered. Because my aunt had cranked up the heat inside, Walt took off his shirt. I noticed that thin white mushrooms were taking over his back, like a milky fur. They moved in a lazy wave as he worked the hammer.

"Can I touch them?" I asked.

"Sure," he said. He dug out nutmeat and let the hazelnut shells pile up on the floor. My aunt came out of the kitchen to cut a few mushrooms off his back and disappeared again to use them in her dish. They were velvety and blooming. I could feel them growing under my fingertips. I plucked one.

"Does it hurt?" I asked.

"No," he said.

"What does it feel like?" I asked.

"It's a tingling sensation," he said, "like I'm forgetting something."

"They're growing fast," my aunt said as she came out of the kitchen holding plates full of her special burgers: two slices of grilled eggplant with a ground pork and mushroom patty in between. Afterward, my aunt plucked the mushrooms off Walt Suo's back, the way I plucked out white hairs from my father's head. We ate the mushrooms raw.

"I like him very much, but he smells more and more like decay," my aunt told me over tea the next morning after he departed. She had a collection of tea balls that blossomed into floral arrangements when placed in hot water. One was opening up and spreading its petals in a clear glass teapot.

. . .

My aunt trained me on the usual gua sha procedures so that I could run the parlor myself on the days that she wanted to spend with Walt Suo. Most of the customers that were accustomed to my aunt treated me informally because I was much younger than them. They had big watches and demanded glasses of water in gruff voices. They distrusted my style, complaining that I was not as good as my aunt.

I could sense the disappointment in my aunt's customers when they saw that it was just me in the parlor and my aunt was nowhere in sight. She had many admirers. Every so often, one of them would leave a gift for me to deliver to her: a hen quivering in a rice sack or a giant fish wrapped in wax paper. I learned that it was not unusual for somebody to be smoking in the alley, waiting for her, as we locked up the parlor. I knew they had no chance dating her. She had a specific type.

. . .

One day, a customer I had worked with came back to the parlor to show me what had happened to his back. It had sprouted a hawthorn bush. I couldn't believe my eyes. Spring was the season of the hawthorn fruit, red and tangy. Street vendors strung them onto bamboo skewers and then coated them in a sugar glaze. These sweets were called tang hulu and reminded me of my childhood. "You did this," he said. I fed him all the lines my aunt used. "This is nothing to worry about," I said. "Didn't you want something like this to happen?" I took him into the private room and trimmed his growth. Over our private grooming sessions, I grew fond of him.

We went for walks around the reservoir to discuss his progression. Vendors sold tang hulu all along the route. My customer went by the name 'Rick,' the name he gave himself in an English class long ago. He had a habit of plucking handfuls of edible things from the trees around the reservoir and giving them to me to taste. For a long time after our very last walk together, I would find old berries in my pockets.

The longer I worked with Rick, the harder it was to tame the wilderness on his back. As I groomed, nature kept flourishing and solidifying on his body to a point where I'd tug at a growth or snip at a branch and Rick would cry out in pain or lose his mind for a moment. I learned from my aunt that nature would eventually take over each man in bloom. It was just a matter of time. We talked about it at night, when it was just the two of us.

. . .

It happened to Walt Suo. His decay could not be ignored. I watched his body disappear as his mushrooms thrived. He was so completely covered in them that I could barely make out his face. My aunt and I accompanied him on a trip to the mountains, where his ancestors lived, where he burned paper money for them every Lunar New Year. It was where he wanted to spend eternity.

On the drive, I read Ovid's *Metamorphosis* in between naps. People turned into birds, stones, spiders, stars, and even mountain ranges. I thought about how my aunt would like it and made a note to look for a copy in Chinese. I looked out the window often. It was remarkable how every bit of land was used for some purpose. No wonder plants had begun to sprout from the backs of our men, I thought. Slogans painted on bright red banners on the hills stood out in the landscape. They asked the people to protect the environment and to be good stewards of the land.

We wound around the mountainsides on narrow ledges where it seemed like we would slip off the edge into a canyon. Soon, the air began to smell like medicine, and vistas of terraced mountainsides opened up to us. When we made it to our destination, a small village in a bowl between two mountain peaks, we shared an egg and tomato dish with rice and grilled meats on sticks. Walt Suo explained to us that the people who lived in the area were a matriarchal people. The women went out every day to pick mushrooms and tend to the earth while the men took care of domestic tasks. We took a walk by the river and saw elderly women carrying bloated baskets on their backs, scaling down the mountains faster than any of us could.

When we hiked up the trail the next day, the clouds moved fast and close, their shadows passing over the mountainsides. Halfway up, Walt Suo lost the ability to use his legs, so my aunt and I had to carry him. He was surprisingly light, as if he'd been hollowed out, filamentous fibers replacing his insides. It was almost dusk when we'd found a clearing for Walt Suo, right where the mountain path curved into shadow and turned into a whole different ecosystem. Goats stood at impossible angles on the cliffs above us. "Right here," he said. "I remember this exact place."

It was getting dark. My aunt and I pitched a tent off to the side of the trail. We set Walt Suo down in a patch of grass under a tree at the edge of a cliff, so that he could look out at the view. From our place in the tent, Walt Suo looked like mushrooms growing from a wet log in the moonlight. My aunt and I left the next morning.

• • •

There is a square in my aunt's village that is spacious and beautiful and for the people. It is lit by multicolored streetlights. I went to it often as a child, hoping something exciting would happen. Street vendors sell desserts, and children climb on monuments of old war heroes. People run laps around it. Groups gather for qi gong. Elderly women perform coordinated dance steps to music played over tinny speakers. They wave colorful fans and sequined rags around in the air. Beyond the square is an elementary school and a small park, and beyond that small park is Rick.

The thing about men in bloom is that once you begin to love them, they become a horizon. A bamboo forest. An orchard of fruit trees. A beautiful still pond, full of lilies and their glowing blossoms. In their new bodies, they live forever, but they aren't yours. The last time I saw Rick, he was all back, his body weighed down with fruit. He was beautiful. We sat at a bench for a long time before picking out a little patch of ground for him to root. I held his hand, which was the last soft thing to go.

I visited him frequently that spring and watched him spread far and wide. Children discovered him and picked his berries. At the end of spring, he started to wilt from heat. He released all his berries and they stuck to the bottoms of my shoes. I picked leaves from Rick's hawthorn bush to remember him by.

On the night I was packing to go home, I showed Rick's leaves to my aunt. She walked over to her bed. It was a hard unyielding thing, like sleeping on a flat slate of rock dynamited out of a quarry, but it was a traditional bed that my aunt and all my older relatives were used to. She lifted the bedsheets off of it. I noticed a faint line that split the frame perfectly in half. At the base of the bed, there was a hasp, like on a jewelry box. When she lifted the swing latch, the bed opened up like a nut.

Inside of it were impressions of all her men, various textures rubbed with soft blue pencil strokes onto thin white paper. She must have made them while they slept beside her. An abundance of mushroom rubbings sat at the top of her collection. We added a rubbing of Rick's leaf to the pile. As I stood there watching my aunt close the bed before me, I performed gua sha on my life. It bloomed before me with meaning. I saw indications of distress and signs of healing, where the redness was less strong than before. I wondered how long or short I would live, who I would let in, and how I would be changed.

SOFT BREAST MECHANISM

I once was a plant nurse. Plants were in fashion because they added a splash of color to an office. I went from office to office with a watering can, all the way up to the fifty-sixth floor, spending the most time in the executive suites because the executives had the plants that were the toughest to care for, plants that were breathtakingly grand but finicky. I had to tap a little electronic scanner against the barcodes taped to all the plants under my care so that there was a record somewhere that they were visited and tended to.

Horace took care of all the office pets. Animals were in fashion because they added a splash of life to an office. Fish were the most popular. He had the harder job. These were living things with brains: fish, lizards, hamsters, and chinchillas. He had to feed all of them and check on their water. He had to make sure they didn't chew through things and accidentally get electrocuted.

Carnivorous plants lived in a crimson corporate negotiation chamber on the very top floor of the skyscraper. Venus flytraps and monkey cups lived in elevated terrariums. This was where our paths crossed, Horace's and mine. The Venus flytrap was my responsibility. The monkey cup was his. The Venus flytrap didn't have to consume insects to stay alive. It just needed the usual plant care: light, water, soil, a good conversation. The monkey cups, on the other hand, needed to catch insects in their cups to survive, a cricket every once in a while.

We had the whole place to ourselves Friday afternoons in the summer. This was where Horace wooed me, in the clean aftermath of the departure of the executives. Sometimes Horace would hold my head in his hands and massage it, which was a service he often performed for the animals. I'd read to him from my stash of adventure novels the way I read to the finicky plants. (It is scientifically proven that they respond better to the sound of the female voice.) We pilfered imported chocolates from the candy dishes until the executives started hiding them from us.

·   ·   ·

For the longest time, ever since I was a girl, I had a problem with insomnia. I couldn't remember the feeling of a good night's sleep. There was an incident when I was young. I woke up in the middle of a winter night to the face of a stranger staring into mine. He disappeared through the open front door as I screamed for my parents. Who was that man?

I did not miss sleep at first. In my childhood home, I collected hair from the carpeted floors and shaped the strands into figurines when I was supposed to be sleeping. My first figurine was a bunny sculpted out of hair and dust and lint. My hair gathering became a habit: at sleepovers in strange homes, in motel rooms, in the wilderness surrounding a tent. I grew my hair to my waist, infused it with olive oils and honey, and brushed it with one thousand strokes every evening. Whenever I changed residences, my hair figurines came with me. By the time I met Horace, I'd collected two suitcases full of them.

. . .

After work, Horace drove us back to our office in Chinatown where we deposited our equipment. He sometimes invited me out for the rest of the afternoon. We ate steamed pork buns, got our hair trimmed on a balcony, and did our shopping. We purchased supplies in Chinatown because they were cheap. After getting the plant food, we searched for the live stuff: cockroaches for the lizards, crickets for the bearded dragon and the monkey cups, mice for the snakes. Horace kept them alive at his apartment until they were needed at work. Our final stop in Chinatown was always for the anchovies. Horace knew a vendor who set up her station on the sidewalk and sat on a stool all day with a fan in her hand. She wore a straw hat and flowery kitchen pants. Five plastic washtubs surrounded her, and inside each washtub were slippery swirls of anchovies and ribbonfish in water. The fish came in all sizes, some as small as fingernails and some like ouroboros circling into themselves to fit. We selected anchovies out of a washtub, and she plopped them in a plastic bag full of water that Horace balanced on his lap as he drove me home.

When Horace stayed over on certain evenings, I'd pretend to drift off to sleep beside him as I'd done with lovers in the past, waiting until he fell into a deep sleep before slipping out from under his arm to do what I'd always done.

His hairs were thick, black, and gleaming.

. . .

The anchovies we carefully selected were for the catfish. Horace's toughest client was a celebrity, a chef. In his office, one huge catfish named Ivan drifted alone in a large tank that glowed a rich Yves Klein blue. I called it the isolation chamber, an empty landscape for one lone fish to do what it wished. The tank, though wide, was very narrow. Ivan's whiskers brushed against the glass as he swam. Horace had to climb up a stepladder to reach the top of the tank so that he could toss each flapping anchovy into the water. Ivan prowled at his slow pace, sucked a few anchovies into his vacuum cleaner mouth, and then casually joined the uneaten ones for a swim around the tank until his next fit of hunger. At the end of those feedings, Horace and I remained, eating peaches. We turned off the light and let the blue of the tank illuminate the room.

. . .

I was working on an effigy of a miner in Colorado one night using a mix of my and Horace's hair when I found him standing over me, rubbing his eyes.

"Come back to bed," he said.

I was looping my long hairs around his short ones to make a shovel. I shook my head. "I can't sleep," I said. "You go ahead."

He refused. He pulled me back into bed, telling me he had a remedy for sleeplessness, something he'd learned as an apprentice in a Chinese medicine treatment center.

"You can try," I said, "but it won't work on me." I crawled into bed with him. He slipped his hand under my right breast, squeezing in a rhythm, kneading it like an expert bread maker. The rhythm seemed familiar. I tried to discern it.

. . .

I woke up at dawn weeping, having slept for the first time in years. I couldn't make myself stop. We all learned at some point that our brains process things in sleep. For me, there must have been a lot in the queue, a line of anchovies waiting to be chomped by my catfish-brain. Horace told me the tempo at which he squeezed my breast matched the song "Staying Alive."

I asked Horace to come over every evening. All I ever wanted to do was sleep. With him around, my eyesight improved, I became more beautiful, I lost ten pounds, I grew four inches. Horace had firm but soft feminine hands: That's the only part of him I still picture from time to time. I loved those hands.

. . .

I noticed that the plants at work began to look healthier after my rounds, as if I gained something during sleep that the plants needed, a processed spirit that energized them. I thought their improved states would demonstrate that I deserved a raise or some words of affirmation.

One day I walked into the building to find these timed spritzers everywhere wetting the plants at the appropriate hours. Automatic feeders had been attached to the cages of the office pets spitting out a pellet or two at measured time increments. The celebrity chef cooked Ivan when he had important French visitors one weekend. Building management had hired consultants looking to find ways to save money. We were let go.

Newly unemployed, I just wanted to catch up on sleep and lose myself in labyrinthine dreams. But I had trouble with Horace's hands. They would grow lazy, jolting me out of sleep, or he would simply not be in the mood. For some time, he chain smoked by the kitchen window as he searched the newspaper for new employment. He found another job quickly, working in a different skyscraper. One day, I saw Horace with another woman in Chinatown together and followed them. They performed all the same rituals Horace and I had once done. I had been cleanly replaced.

Sleep left me for a second time, and it was more painful than the first. I wanted that feeling of beginning anew every morning, not the weariness of one long endless life. Sleep was like getting a little taste of death. Life had to be squeezed into the time in between sleeps. The little deaths were important. I grudgingly returned to my hair sculptures.

. . .

Reenacting our old rituals, I wandered through Chinatown on my own late into the night. I was Jeanne Moreau walking through the streets in *Elevator to the Gallows* with the jazz music. I passed the lit-up storefronts of psychics, karaoke taverns, restaurants full of families, trinket shops, and massage parlors. Men smoked in the alleyways next to their motorcycles with their shirts off. Then I saw something, as if it were meant for me: a neon sign advertising a *soft breast mechanism* glowed against a shop window right above the storefront of a foot massage parlor.

I climbed the stairs. The room smelled like medicine. A woman in a stiff white suit that looked like a karate outfit pointed me to a testing chamber. All the apparatuses reminded me of a doctor's office. I had to take off my shirt and my bra and lie down on a small bed. A gloved hand appeared from a hole in the wall, holding a different mechanism each time. There were many soft breast mechanisms to try, in varying color schemes, all with a different pulse to them. I hummed "Staying Alive" against each soft breast mechanism until I found one with a pulse that matched.

"Will you be purchasing the detachable robotic arm as well?" the woman asked as I walked up to the checkout counter with my selection.

I nodded.

She went into the back room and procured a kit that enabled me to screw a metallic appendage into the wall above my bed. "This will hold the soft breast mechanism in place," she said.

. . .

If someone were to ask me if there was anything I'd run back into a burning house to save, it would be my suitcases of hair, if only for all the midnight hours spent collecting in the silence.

When I returned home with my new purchase, I unzipped my suitcases and waded through my collection. My figurines contained hair from my mother and father, all my lovers, the animals I've had, all the people who occupied my life or slipped by unnoticed at some time. A human being sheds up to one hundred strands of hair a day. Every strand belonged to someone once.

I wanted to mimic all the conditions for sleep that I'd learned from Horace. I amassed my hair figurines into one giant humanoid and laid it beside me. Then I considered my new purchase. The soft breast mechanism came in a beautiful clamshell box with a bone clasp that slid into and out of a red loop. I opened the box, took out the object, and set it in the flexible arm that I'd attached to the wall. It swooped over me just like a lover's would in the spooning position. In that manner, I found a sleep all my own.

SKIN SUIT

My parents are membranes of light. They are more magnificent than the Aurora Borealis or a rare tube of color that appears in a meteor shower. They travel together like the iridescent wings on a dragonfly.

There is a bright body-shaped hole the size of me that forms when they intersect, which lasts maybe two weeks out of the year. That is when I take my vacation from the factory. I travel northward, to my birthplace, and wait for them in a belly boat adrift on a glacial lake.

That is where I am now.

It is quiet here, and the water is so still, it is as if I am puttering through empty space. I can smell bears in the periphery. It has been a long time since my last visit, and I've forgotten how dramatic my parents' arrival is. When I see their overlapping membranes descend from the sky, the entire landscape brightens and flares. I enter through the shape of me.

· · ·

I am a lump of matter. My parents pushed me out into the world through this same intersecting shape twenty-nine years ago. I was surprisingly solid and heavy and fell fast toward the earth. (It is hard to predict what two membranes of light might conceive.)

Nearby, two women lived inside a log cabin surrounded by glaciers. My parents' trail of light led me to the front doorstep of the cabin. My parents conveyed to the two women my story as best they could: a light display over my body.

One of these women researched weather patterns and had been studying my parents her entire life, despite other scientists declaring her efforts to be misplaced. The other was an excellent hunter and taxidermist. The women referred to me as a blob baby. They doted on me even though they did not know what I was. I had a malleable shape and dark lumpy appendages that could bend and fold and twist in all directions.

The researcher, whose name was Janelle, tracked my parents' annual arrival to the glacial lake and forecasted their visits one hundred years into the future based on her exhaustive calculations and notes. When the time of their arrival came, she took me to the edge of the lake to wait for them until I was old enough to do it on my own. My parents always came as Janelle predicted. *They operate under a larger, stricter law*, Janelle explained to me, her slouchy frame huddled over her weather reports and star charts.

The taxidermist, whose name was Ravenna, attended taxidermy conventions and learned the best methods for remolding dead skin and brought home many awards. For every birthday, she gave me a skin suit that molded me into a human shape that resembled her. Each year, the suit was a little bigger and more precise in craftsmanship. When I looked into the mirror, I admired the beauty of the female form.

. . .

I leave the skin suit in the belly boat in order to fit into the opening created by my parents. From where I stand, I can see that the suit is very worn from use, and I am filled with a sort of sadness. It looks like a dead body without me in it. The red color of the lips has faded away. I have not replaced the suit since I was twenty-five. That was the year Ravenna died.

· · ·

When Ravenna died, I took all the animal skins lying around in her studio. I experimented with the form of ravens, bears, wolves, red foxes, and caribou and considered the possibility of living as something else. I roamed around the wilderness filling the inside of these dead animals until Janelle found me as a marmot in an alpine meadow, disoriented and hungry. Back at the cabin, she helped me back into the human skin suit I left behind.

That year, I chose not to meet my parents and went on an expedition over the glaciers toward the ocean instead. I planned to push westward until I'd destroyed the skin suit or it fell apart in strips around me. But it was surprisingly resilient, a testament to Ravenna's hand. When I reached the ocean, I loved its bound-lessness. I constructed a lean-to on a steep cliff overlooking the water and mended the skin suit the way Ravenna taught me. On that trip, I learned that I could not help clinging tightly to the forms I love. For instance: hands. I love the shape of hands.

· · ·

Inside the intersection of their membranes, my parents communicate with me through light displays. My foreparent's speech is heavy with yellows and my hindparent's with aquamarines. Together, they speak a botanical green. My foreparent's yellow light pales and brightens in predictable arcs, but her brightest emanation—radiant as the sun—is rare. She is capable of harsh, ugly light, a yellow that sickens skin or uncovers all of your flaws, but it is also rare. My hindparent's light can be unpredictable, calm one moment and tumultuous the next. Her most angry emanations are soft and edgeless, but her deep blue articulations of sadness can be pulsating and immense like the ocean itself. Though they are genderless, I refer to my parents as if they are women because of Janelle and Ravenna.

I like watching my parents speak to each other in their majestic displays of communication that light up the earth. I cannot talk to them in their language and often wonder about all that is lost between us. My understanding of their emanations is limited, as is their understanding of me.

They tell me about the wonders and places they've seen: the alignment of the planets and stars, the animal migrations and tree growths, the state of the arctic deserts sitting on beds of permafrost, the polar ice caps. Their perspective is colossal. They know nothing about the sudden panic that sometimes grips me in the middle of the night and makes me sprint out of the factory grounds into an open field, unzip my body suit, and heave deep breaths of nothing. Where does that come from?

On this visit, I spend the pale moments examining the boundary where my parents intersect, the patterns made by the overlapping of their membranes. I walk in circles staring at the perimeter until I feel dizzy. When I was younger, I entered the bright body-shaped hole the size of me with things hidden in the folds of my lump and proceeded to decorate the boundary walls with framed pictures, paintings, and small pieces of nature. As I've grown older, I study the places where the walls are bare: the intersecting pattern of the boundary that made me.

· · ·

When it is time to leave, I consider the lake in its stillness. The light upon it changes as my parents separate and the opening closes. My belly boat looks like a donut resting on a blue table. Back when Ravenna was alive, this would have been the moment I retired my latest skin suit. There would be another one waiting for me at home, wrapped in a red ribbon. But this time I won't be getting any replacements. My old skin suit hangs over the edge of the belly boat. I rest it on top of me for a long time, the way one would lay an outfit over one's body in front of a mirror, and then I spread it out flat over the water. I watch it slowly sink toward the bottom of the lake, letting go of the hands last. I look around me for another form. A mountain, a green meadow covered in flowers, a pristine lake so calm it is like a body of light.

SOMETHING CLOSE

The Claw broke again, and when the repairman came to look at it, he left a large brown stain on my bedroom rug, which he came back the next day to clean.

My house was in shambles. While the repairman sang along to opera music and rubbed the stain out upstairs, woodworkers downstairs stripped the rooms to their frameworks and cut wood beams with power saws and lathes. I was remodeling on a grand scale. After spending several years abroad in different cities, I didn't want to travel anymore. I wanted to put down roots.

I had recently come into some money and decided to put it all into transforming this house into a miniature replica of a castle I had seen on an ocean cliff in Wales. Things I wanted: secret passageways, dumbwaiters, long hallways with suits of armor bathed in moonlight, towers to sleepwalk into. Workers came in and out of the house at all hours to make this happen. If I wanted quiet surroundings, I had to go outside.

It was a brisk autumn day. I rang the doorbell of my dog-walking client two houses away from mine to pick up Trudee at the appointed hour. Living in the gated community of Forest Manor Estates, where giant multi-story houses loomed over sprawling green lawns, many of the homeowners kept pets. I had a couple of dog-walking clients in the neighborhood. I didn't have any pets of my own; I felt that a short moment of camaraderie was enough. The key to extracting the purity of companionship was to keep the experience fleeting, so that you were always wanting more.

"Here, Trudee," I called. I heard the click clack of her paws on the linoleum before she appeared in the doorway. Her big mastiff tongue licked my face wet.

I drove us to a wooded area nearby with a park and lots of intersecting trails. I followed the whims of Trudee the dog. She tugged me toward a large tree and burrowed through its long and low-hanging branches, leaving a flurry of red leaves in her wake. I followed. We were in a domed sanctuary at the base of the tree. Trudee marked her territory. Following her lead, I unzipped my fly and relieved myself. Trudee began to bark. I saw, just beyond the leaves, an old man sitting on a bench looking at us.

I paid him no mind. Trudee and I chose a path into the woods that approached the playground and then curved around a small body of water, looping back around to where we started. When we returned, the old man was still there on his bench.

"What were you doing back there by that tree?" the old man asked.

"Oh, just following the dog," I said. "Her name's Trudee."

"Don't mean to interfere," he said, "but you're supposed to exert some control on her. I've been watching you lurch after that dog like some kind of fool."

I looked down at Trudee. She was tugging again. I kept my hand in a tight fist around the leash to keep her in place. I looked back at the man. "Oh, she's fine," I said. "This is nothing I can't handle." I listed off my experience. "Sometimes I walk five or six dogs at once."

The old man started to laugh. He pointed at Trudee. Her snout had found its way to a bike rack, and she had immediately started to chew on a bicycle seat. I tried to pull her away, but she had a stubborn, unbudging neck. The old man laughed again and looked out toward the water.

The seat seemed custom-made, wider and more donut-shaped than the generic kind. I could tell by its size that the bicycle belonged to a child. I searched for the owner. There was a big group of boys playing in the field next to the water. They tossed around a boomerang, and I watched as it flew out over the water and then curved back for someone to catch. I beckoned over to them while pointing at the bike. "Whose is this?" I shouted.

A boy came running. He had very big ears. "No, no, no, no, no," he shouted when he saw the remnants of his bike seat.

I told him, "I'm sorry, I can replace it." All I had was a credit card and a pocketful of change. "I can send you a check if you give me your address."

I searched my body for a pen, but the boy was already shaking his head. "I can't give you that information," he said. "You're a stranger."

"If you wait here," I said, "I can run home and write one to you right away."

"How do I know you'll come back?" he said.

"I don't have enough cash on me," I said, giving him a look of defeat.

"You could get me another bike," he said.

The old man looked up from his reading. He said, "There's a Walmart just over there." He gestured toward the parking lot and let out another laugh.

"I know where the Walmart is," I said. I lifted the kid and the bicycle and Trudee onto the back of my truck—he wanted to sit with the dog—and I sat alone in the front. As we cleared the park, I looked in the rearview mirror. Something caught in my throat. With the dog and the boy sitting there gazing back at me, it felt something close to having a family.

I drove slowly. I looked into the rearview mirror and watched the boy run his fingers through Trudee's fur. I pulled up to the Walmart logo. The star had been moved, from between the "L" and the "M" to between the "M" and the "A" by some fault of the lettering guy. As we walked from the parking lot into the store, I told the boy I was just going to take him in to choose a new seat, a quick in and out.

He said, "In order to replace a bike seat on this bike, you have to get it custom ordered. My mother ordered one for me after a crook stole my first one. She paid more than the cost of this entire bike for it. I think it's best if you purchase me a brand new bike. It would be cheaper for you."

I asked him, "Where did you learn how to negotiate like that?"

He said, "It's just what makes the most sense. Sometimes it's harder to replace a part than a whole. That bike seat was one-of-a-kind."

I nodded. "Okay," I said. "Whatever."

· · ·

We walked through the sliding doors and were hit with a blast of cold air. This Walm*art seemed different than other Walmarts I'd been to, colder. First, we had to walk past a long row of vending machines. There was something odd about them. In one, a woman stood frozen in a block of ice. She wore a lacy white gown, and her body hovered in a frozen prism of ice in the space where soft drinks usually sat. We studied her for a minute and then kept walking toward the aisle of bicycles for sale. The price tags were all facedown by default and the kid flipped the price tags over to read them as he stopped at each bicycle. He tried out a couple of bicycles, making a loop through sporting goods, bedding, girls' clothing, electronics, pet food, toys, and back. I took Trudee for a brisk stroll through the aisles. Lit by fluorescent lights, each aisle extended before us. We strolled past the cylindrical containers full of rubber fitness balls, the minimalist aisles of health food in sleek packages, and the glowing corner with glass displays of electronic doohickeys no bigger than my pinky nail. The boy rode past Trudee and me on a different bike each time we saw him.

The boy finally chose one: a metallic blue bike with matching metallic blue pedals, a white bike seat, and octagonal reflectors.

"This one's $79," I said.

He shrugged. "It's on sale," he said.

"The seat's not even that good," I said.

"I like the color," he said. He pressed his finger into the seat so that it dimpled in the middle.

As we pushed the bike toward the cash register, we passed the woman frozen in ice, and at the checkout line, the boy's face changed, and he said, "The woman scared me."

I didn't answer for a moment. It seemed that this was my opportunity to be fatherly, so I thought about what to do. I bent down next to him and said, "Well, we can look at her again. We should look at the woman in the ice until we are no longer afraid."

The boy nodded and took my hand. We retraced our steps and stood there looking at the woman in the ice, like she was a painting in a gallery.

She was positioned like a figurehead on a ship. She had white frost around her eyes, which were half-open, and I could see each individual eyelash sealed in a crystal of water. Fat icicles had formed around clumps of what appeared to be long black hair. Her long lacy white gown was elegant like a wedding dress, but not nearly as formal, more like something meant for a picnic in a field of flowers or for sleeping.

"My mother," the boy said, "had me when she was forty. She had me through artificial insemination."

"Your mom told you this?" I asked.

"Yes," he said. "She never found love. That's what she told me." The boy stared hard at the woman in the ice, his own reflection imposed on the woman; after some time, he looked more at ease. "I'm going to try really hard to find it."

He left me to stare at the ice by myself. Trudee started whimpering, growing impatient. I looked up at the woman one last time. What was she made of?

. . .

"Could I get a horn?" the boy said. He held up a mini trumpet attached to a red rubber device, sealed in plastic.

"I don't owe you anything else," I said.

He looked down at the horn and did not move. "You could be kind," he said.

I wheeled the bike to the cash register, and the boy followed me closely, stepping on my heels and holding tightly onto his new horn. After I paid, I asked the elderly lady at the cash register about the woman in the soda machine. Her eyes met mine with disinterest.

"If you want to purchase the woman in the soda machine, you just have to deposit the correct amount of money," she said. "Haven't you ever used a vending machine before?"

"I don't understand," I said.

The cashier let out a groan and picked up her cane. She flicked her light off and hobbled over to the soda machine. She pointed at the numbers above the bill and coin slots. "It's fifty cents," she said, tapping the plastic. She hobbled back to her station and turned her light back on. I dug into my pocket. I found two quarters.

Illustrations of sodas decorated the frame of the machine where the frozen woman stood: fizzy lemon, orange, grape, apple, and cherry, whole fruits bursting out of the cans. I put the coins into the machine and pushed the button; there was only one to push. The machine prompted me with questions that I had to answer through a keypad: my age, weight, height, and address. Nothing happened afterward. "Maybe the machine's broken," the boy said. I gave the frozen woman one last look, and then we left.

. . .

"You can drop me off here," the boy said when we returned to the park. I helped the boy out of the back of my truck and then brought down his new bicycle. As I watched the boy disappear into the woods, the old man, still on the bench, pointed at me and chuckled.

The boy left his old bicycle in the back of my truck. I ripped the remains of the seat off to let Trudee have it, but feeling the texture of it myself for the first time, I brought it with me into the cab to take a closer look. The seat was lumpy. I peered into the tear, and inside it, there were wooden beads nested between layers of memory foam. The seat itself smelled of animal hide, and when I pushed against it, it contoured to my hand, like an airplane pillow. Attached to the corner of the seat, there was a tag with a website written on it. "Interesting kid, that one, spoiled by his mother," I said, looking into Trudee's eyes through my rearview mirror. Behind me, the sky was divided almost perfectly in half, as rain clouds moved in.

Trudee's owner was not home when I rang his doorbell, so I brought Trudee back to my place. Scaffolds surrounded my house like fencing. When we entered, it was quiet; four wood-workers sat around the island in my kitchen with their feet up on the counters. They passed around a bag of grapes. A fifth worker was handling a live fish flopping in the sink. I told them on their first day that they could make themselves comfortable in my house because they were in for a lot of work.

They saw me come through the door and waved. Trudee ran toward them, pushing her giant body against each of their legs.

I asked, "Is it safe to take a look around?"

Martin pressed down on the fish firmly with both hands before he addressed me. "Sure, though you won't want to lean on anything."

I walked around the house. It had been transformed, opened up. Afternoon light flooded in through the windows, and I felt for a moment that there was light inside of my body. There was a hole in the center of the ceiling, and I could see straight up into a tower of scaffolding; this was where the spire would eventually go. My shipment of iron grills for the windows had come in, I noticed; they had not yet been installed. I went back into the kitchen and asked Pete about them.

"We weren't sure you still wanted them," he said. "They would dramatically affect the light."

"In the castles in Wales," I explained, "the windows are not just for light; they had to be built thinking also of defense. I'd like to stick to the plan."

I went upstairs to my room to check on the Claw. The repair-man was gone; the stain was gone. The Claw looked correct. I laid the rice-stuffed dummy, a replica of myself, flat into the launcher and pressed the red button on the side of the machine. It slammed the dummy into the air. My prototype flew upwards fifteen feet—I had high ceilings—and landed in my bed. The target projection was right on track. Last time, the Claw had thrown the thing straight into the floor, and the rice had spilled all over the place. That could've been me.

Now, the dummy lay serenely on my bed. I inserted my body into the launcher and closed my eyes. Some days, I got into the Claw facedown, and other days face up. I got in facedown and pushed the button. I felt my body rise into the air, hovering just for a moment, and then I twisted my body over and landed with my face in my pillow. My bed lurched like a stomach and flung my body upward again. Then, it lurched me up a second time. Some nights, it takes quite a few launches from the Claw to get me to sleep.

I turned on the computer and searched for the manufacturer of the boy's bike seat. It was called a Bikfort. I read through a full explanation of yin and yang forces at work beneath the outer contours of its donuty shape. It seemed like an object of love and care, and I had this feeling that the boy's new purchase was going to upset his mother.

The doorbell rang. Trudee barked. Her barks were piercing and anxious. I walked down the stairs. The woodworkers were gathered around the kitchen island, making a commotion. Martin's voice: "Mind if I take some of this home for my wife to try? Don't think I've cooked a better fish." There were sounds of assent. I peeked in. It looked like a birthday party. I could see a banner out of the corner of my eye, for Pete. A giant fish laid out on a long oval plate sat at the center of the kitchen table. I lingered behind the wall separating the kitchen from the hallway, peering at my workers. When the doorbell rang a second time, I made my way to the door.

. . .

A woman stood there holding a red purse as small as a lip, only big enough to fit two quarters snugly. I recognized her instantly. "We have thirty minutes of time," she said.

I asked her how she found me.

"You gave me your address," she said. Her voice was just a little fried and reminded me of the buzzing light bulb in the basement of my house. She was wet from defrosting or the rain. Her white gown clung to her body and had become translucent. Trudy burrowed her snout into the woman's crotch, and the woman laughed. I welcomed her inside. We sat on the living room couch. Trudee rested her body on the woman's feet.

"What can I do for you?" I asked.

She said, "There's not very much time for formalities." She got up and walked around me. I noticed a wet spot on the couch. The woodworkers sat around the kitchen table and ate their fish. They had a clear view of everything. Even if they were minding their own business, I wanted privacy.

I led the woman up to my room. We lay next to each other on the bed looking at the ceiling. The Claw stood gleaming in the corner. She said, "I'm here to make love to you." She rethought what she had already said. "I mean, half of me wants to do that. But the other half craves other things."

"What are those things?" I asked.

"Closeness, excitement, companionship," she said.

"Why were you in that machine?" I asked.

"I chose the ice machine option," she said. She explained how it worked. When her body was idle, the machine kept her frozen in time. When her body was summoned into the world, she could defrost and experience everything she craved in a short burst of intensity.

"To keep the experience fleeting," I said.

"Yes," she said, "exactly."

She stroked Trudee with her toes. "What is that?" she asked. She pointed at the Claw.

"That is the Claw," I said.

"Can I try it?" she asked.

I shook my head. "It is only calibrated to my weight and size. If anyone else got in, they'd risk severe injury."

She wanted me to show her how it worked, so I gave her a demonstration. I launched myself, facedown, and landed solidly in the center of my bed. She clapped her hands and inched toward the Claw. Before I could stop her, she had crawled into the launcher herself and pressed the button. I watched in horror as she flew in an arch right over the bed, right over me, and hit the wall, leaving a wet mark that looked more like a splatter. She jumped up and laughed, though her lip was bleeding. She spat out a tooth. I rushed over to her. I led her into my bathroom and sat her on my toilet lid. I dabbed at her lip until the beads of blood stopped forming. I cleaned off her tooth and put it in her pocket. She walked out of the bathroom, and I followed her.

Because she was set on knowing the feel, we moved the Claw until the change in trajectory would compensate for her size. When she pushed the button on the launcher, I waited near my bed, ready to catch her in my own arms. She moved the Claw according to where she landed each time. And with one final try, she landed directly in the center of the bed.

"Turn off the lights and lie on top of me," she said. She hiked up her white dress. I switched off the light and came to her. She was still, facedown on the bed.

In the darkness, I climbed on top. My body covered hers like a shell. Her bare skin was smooth and cold underneath. When I entered her, I started sweet-talking into her ear. She told me to stop. She said, "I get more pleasure from lip-sounds than words. Just talk silently if you don't mind." I obeyed and only moved my lips. I could hear them parting and pressing together. I thought about what I was saying, which wasn't really coherent, and felt self-conscious, so I stopped altogether.

"Keep talking," she said.

I took a deep breath and continued to move my lips to words

I thought in my head. As she moaned softly beneath me, my sweet talk had somehow turned into a confession of my loneliness and fears, until I finally came. She fell asleep beneath me. Sniffing the back of her ear, I thought it smelled of that dampness found in flooded cellars, the smell of age-old items in storage. I could feel her bones through the dress. Not wanting to wake her, I stayed where I was and let my mind drift. I felt like I'd fallen into some current, hadn't really known what I'd done in the interval of fumbling, only that I'd never be the same.

As our thirty minutes came to a close, the woman woke up. She slipped out from under me and picked up her tiny lip purse, empty, from the table. She'd left a damp feeling on my sheets. I followed her downstairs, rubbing my eyes. Everywhere around us: a film of dust and a smell of timber. The kitchen was clean, the table cleared. Two woodworkers remained. They groaned under their loads of beams as they transferred them from the porch to the kitchen. I watched her slip away in the dark.

. . .

I felt so much desire in her wake as I stood on the porch and waited for my heart to slow down. I saw a light turn on at Trudee's house, and minutes later, Trudee's owner came over to retrieve her. I watched her run toward her owner with a crazed devotion. I envied that a little bit.

I made myself a sandwich. I wondered if I had enough information on the woman to build a prototype, if she would be at Walm*art next time. Next time, I thought, I'll wait at home for her with flowers, an X drawn on the floor with chalk where the Claw would go for me and another X for her. We'd get thrown into each other, colliding in the most intense way.

The watermarks were already disappearing, from the couch, from my bedroom floor, from my sheets. The Bikfort bike seat sat on my computer desk trickling little beads onto the floor like a waterfall. I noticed that the woman had left behind a small brochure about the "Ice Machine Option." I slipped into the Claw to prepare for sleep. Before I launched myself, I noticed a tiny, barely perceptible bleach stain in the carpet where the previous stain had been. I made a mental note to call the repairman in the morning and then shut my eyes, tight.

CAZENAVE

When I was a young woman, I existed in possibility, just out-side of experience. I studied time. I lived in an international house on Rue de Reuilly in Paris with my dachshund. I enjoyed the company of genteel older men, like Cazenave. We ran up and down the Coulee Vert, an elevated rail line converted into a trail, in the mornings. He'd wait for me by the Jardin de Reuilly wearing his white sports suit, shiny and freshly ironed, reading a newspaper. In the summertime, gnats multiplied and flew in thick clouds along the running path. Breathing through our noses, we jogged toward the Bastille, past the police station and the apartment windowsills full of potted flowers, past the rose gardens and the smells of baking bread below. I ran slightly behind Cazenave because he was taller. My legs were short and my dachshund didn't like running; I had to sort of drag her. The gnats would swirl around us and get tangled in my eye-brows and in Cazenave's mustache, because he was taller. We'd have to sit down on a bench afterward and pick the tiny gnats out of our hairs.

When the air moistened and the gnat population grew gauzy, we knew that it would soon rain. And when it did, the cooler weather cleared out the gnats for a day. Even in the rain, Cazenave waited for me in the same place, umbrella in hand. He was a very skillful runner, hovering his umbrella over the both of us as he marked time with his feet. But under the umbrella, I had to cleave. I was slower (shorter) and my dachshund tired easily in such weather, so on rainy days when we had to move synchronously, I matched Cazenave's breathing pattern, pulled at the dachshund, and picked up my speed to stay under the umbrella, which was always just on the verge of departing. This was the stressful thing about partnership, I thought, the forced synchrony of time. It was on those days that Cazenave talked to me the whole run (about weather, about politics, about his favorite places to vacation—Italy, he said, you must go to Italy) unthreatened by gnats, as I breathed heavily beside him. When we returned to the bench where Cazenave usually waited for me, I sat doubled over myself catching my breath while he stretched his limbs. Sometimes he'd show me pictures on his phone. He thumbed through them really fast, so I couldn't study the faces. He went on many trips. He took advantage of free time.

When the gnats returned to power, Cazenave and I designed experiments to study their movements against ours. One day, I brought two pieces of fly paper with me to the Coulee Vert. Cazenave and I each taped a piece onto our forehead to see if we could catch gnats (many). The next day, Cazenave came with empty wine bottles. We ran holding one in each hand (none). Though they made a wonderful whistling sound against the wind. And even after that, we wanted to understand the effect of a repellent I'd found at the pharmacy, the strongest they had. Cazenave and I rubbed repellent over our limbs until we shined. It was a lazy summer morning, humid as if a rain was due but had not yet come. The gnats were rampant everywhere, so thickly clustered and widely spread that they darkened the environment. Cazenave and I ran into the swarm holding our noses, but we soon realized that the gnats were parting for us. We created tunnels of light in the shapes of our bodies, as if the world had frozen, as if time stood still and allowed us passage all the way down to the Bastille, as if a curtain were opening for us to begin.

. . .

When you look at a bright star through a telescope, you see the star as it was when it was young. Your eye traverses the darkness of time. I was very aware of time in my youth, being a researcher in a lab where experiments on perceptions of time were performed. When Cazenave and I ran together in the rain, I thought about the unbearable pressure of time, in which the bright red umbrella hood hovering above us acted as a symbol of our shared experience, always charging slightly ahead. Cazenave remained constantly on top of a more common Time while I tended to lag behind it. Once, Cazenave scolded me in the rain for being more than one hour late, holding his red umbrella over his head as it poured on me. I adjusted my behavior, but, just like gnats would predictably return to full power until the next rain, my Time would slowly fall further and further behind Cazenave's, in the usual manner. It seemed inevitable that there would be a critical point at which we would begin to drift apart, like two asteroids that, if not meant to collide, would obey the laws of physics and continue on their courses, expanding the distance between them infinitely. Time passed. My dachshund grew old and developed ailments that required my careful attention. I could see Cazenave running in his bright white tracksuit from the window of my room, but when it seemed that the critical point had passed, I no longer tried to meet him. I persisted in solitude.

I saw Cazenave again, years later, in Florence at the Piazza del Duomo, climbing those steep spiraling steps up to the tip of the giant cathedral dome. In the doxological space beneath the dome, an intercom switched on after specific intervals of time and a voice spoke: "Shhh! Silenzio per favore." I suggested that the Italians had programmed the intercom based on how many minutes it took, on average, for sound to crescendo to a noise level that was deemed to be too loud. Cazenave shook his head. "Where is the contact with people?" he said. "Experiments in a vacuum," he said. "That was always your problem." He suggested that there must have been some sort of sound gauge in the space, either a machine or a person, that triggered the recording based on real time. Cazenave's hair was entirely white. At the very top of the Duomo, where we could see all of the city, he told me about the art at the Uffizi, where I had not yet gone, and spoke of the old Byzantine-style paintings that decorated the cathedrals of old, how the artists loved gold paint and flat bodies, whose impossible proportions defied time and space. We pointed at all the narrow alleys and side streets that led the people of Florence to the open piazzas of light. We declared to each other, what bravery, what devotion, what grandeur the human against Time. The bell in the campanile tolled the hour, but I've since forgotten its sound. It was future before it sounded and could not be captured because it had not yet happened; and now it cannot be captured because it is already past.

ACTING LESSONS

When our men came down with a strange sickness, my mother and I took over watching the frog pond. We wore their clothes. The fat growing on our frogs was delicious and in high demand. Thieves often attempted to steal them in the night and resorted to the worst of crimes. We could not afford a break in our vigilance. My mother and I used night vision goggles that our men left behind. A body lurking near the pond would appear as a bright white interference. I moved my hand before my mother's goggles as if it were a dancer on a stage. This amused her for only a short time before she told me to be still.

Not accustomed to being still, I continued to perform for my mother as the leading lady of her night-vision diorama. I twirled and posed, running my hands through my hair as I recited lines I memorized from my mother's old scripts, the words she used to say when she belonged to an acting troupe. She is not an actor anymore.

"Hasn't a daughter the right to protect her dying father from worry and anxiety?" I recited. "Hasn't a wife the right to save her husband's life?"

"You don't know what you're saying," my mother said. She slapped at her face to stay alert.

I yawned. "I'm just going to rest my eyes," I said.

"You must not," she said.

"Then I will perform some more," I said.

"No, you won't." Sometimes, my mother turned into a fortress before my eyes: steely and impenetrable. I wondered what she was protecting.

I was bored out of my mind, and it wasn't even midnight. I stared out in the direction of the pond, where our frogs were coming to life in the night. I could hear them singing.

. . .

For as long as I could remember, we raised cicadas and frogs for profit. They were our livelihood. The best restaurants in the country served them. Once cooked, the cicadas were like nutmeat and the frog fat was rich with the most flavorful oils. Our family business was very lucrative, but my mother had a very different life before.

My mother once traveled across the country with a famous acting troupe. My father was their renowned director. They went from village to village, along the Yellow River, acting out the play, *A Doll's House*, by Henrik Ibsen, in town squares. It was an extremely popular play in our country at the time. Madame Mao herself had once walked across the theater stages of Shanghai as the lead character, Nora.

My mother retired from acting when I was born. My father left her behind in a rural mountain village, where she gave her final performance as Nora. An elderly, childless couple took us in, farmers who lived on a sizeable piece of land at the base of the mountains by the river. When they passed away, it all became ours.

Recently, calamitous floods had struck our land. For some time, our men waded through water up to their waists to get from the timber to the melons to the cicadas to the frogs. A black infection began to spread on their bodies from something poisonous mixing into the water. Now the water was finally receding.

. . .

It was hard to stay alert in the dark with nothing to do. I had trouble keeping my eyes open. "I'm just going to doze for a moment," I said. I closed my eyes.

My mother snapped her fingers in front of my face. "Fine, but not here. If you must sleep, go to the watch house."

I crept through a patch of thick brush as I made my way toward our watch house. Loose debris dangled from tree branches as a result of the floodwaters. I heard the sound of a dog repeatedly dropping a ball onto the floor, but it was only the door to the watch house, opening and closing in the wind. Inside, there was an old bed and tattered sheets faded from rainwater, a kettle rusted open, and a pale human body wrapped in a mantle, its hand clutching a tome titled *The Book of Explanations*, the pages of which were flipping back and forth in the breeze. The body was covered with snails and fungi. I thought it was a sculpture or figurine, but I could still detect its heat with my goggles, the bright flame of life not yet petering. It was like a dormant spirit.

I examined the face that belonged to the body: the eyes closed, the mouth slightly ajar. It looked like my mother's when she was young, like a photograph my mom kept of herself in her jewelry chest.

I pried the heavy book out of the fingers that held it and sifted through it. *The Book of Explanations* was nothing more than an acting manual! It must have belonged to my mother's acting troupe. Every cast had their own manual that guided their lives, hidden somewhere in their encampment. Ours was dusty, worn from age and disuse. Leaving the body behind, I tucked the tome into my satchel and returned to the pond to relieve my mother.

. . .

I read *The Book of Explanations* in a day. It was quiet without our men moving about and chattering outside. I was most engrossed in the section that addressed experiential learning, the subsections of which were "Creation," "Transfiguration," "Departure," and "What to do with the Body in the Mantle." After reading the tome, I was convinced I wanted to give acting a try.

The next night, I feigned sickness at the pond. I groaned and hunched over my belly, complaining of a throbbing pain. My mother, concerned about the recent malaise that afflicted our men, sent me back to my room. As soon as I was out of sight, I ran toward the watch house where the body awaited. The snails and fungi attached to it had doubled overnight. To activate my acting lesson within the experiential section of *The Book of Explanations*, I had to do what the book instructed: I collected the snails from the body and stored them in my satchel; I circled around the mysterious body three times; I ate the fungi from the body until it was clean. The food was much like a sleeping potion, as I felt tired and queasy afterward and immediately fell asleep...

. . .

When I woke, the body was gone. In its place, a thin layer of yellow sediment that blew away in the breeze. It had gotten substantially colder outside. Judging by the color of the sky, it was early morning. The clouds were stacked on top of each other and pressed down on the land. There was a fog over the mirror when I attempted to look into it, obscuring my reflection. I made my way back toward the pond.

When I returned to the pond, in my mother's place lay the dark body of a pig, its translucent ears folded over its glassy eyes, lying in a rumpled pile. The pig had been carved out hollow, its blood dried into lines like a watershed map over bones. I crawled into it, heaving it over my body according to the instructions in *The Book of Explanations*. I wandered to the brook nearby to look at myself. Freshwater fish swam through the current like compact crystals of light, a blurred underwater radiance. Then a peach bobbed in the place where my face should have been. I looked around to find the owner of the peach and heard a voice in the distance.

The landscape was different, emptier and quieter of people. I followed the sound of the voice to the Yellow River. It belonged to this man standing by the river. Once I got close enough to see his features, I recognized him from a picture in Mother's jewelry chest. He was my father, an unmistakable crease across his forehead in the shape of a bird in flight. He climbed upon a rock overlooking the river; he stripped down to his swim shorts; he folded his legs against his wide upper body and cannonballed into the water. He swam beautifully, with command. I walked over toward his things, sniffing them as a pig might. My father looked at me as I looked at him. A long arc of water streamed out of his mouth as he dove back into the river, undisturbed. I glanced into the water to see myself but could see only this: the body of a pig wavering on the surface.

The sky, darkening, blended in with the water so that I could not tell the two apart. A group of people appeared at the shore, darting past me but pausing at the water to put on their suits. Then, they dove in after my father.

"I don't know how to swim," one of the men said, standing fully clothed in water up to his mouth. "This is the farthest I think I can go."

"If our director drowns, if our director catches a nasty bout of pneumonia, you will all be held responsible," a woman from shore shouted in response.

My father was far ahead now. He swam expertly. Back on land, I heard the mechanical murmuring of an engine. A caravan of shiny black cars arrived, followed by a truck loaded with melons in the back, dragging behind it a piano on a three-wheeled platform. I watched the driver hauling the watermelons slink behind his truck. I was hungry. Cloaked in the skin of a pig, I followed the man and watched him devour a small melon. I crept closer to his stash. When he saw me, he shooed me away, throwing his rinds at me. Mud splattered against my coat.

So, this was the land of my father, and this was his cast. He had a loyal entourage, an entire troupe of actors swimming after him to coax him back to shore. "Director, come back!" I heard them scream. "The river water is not yet safe for swimming!" After the floods, the river current was strong. The water was cold and full of garbage and waste. Someone eventually reached my father and dragged him back toward land. The woman remained on the shore, standing at the bank with her arms crossed over her chest. I approached her, wanting a closer look at this leading lady, the one who replaced my mother. When I was close enough to see her face, its perfect soft symmetry, she shoved her foot in my side.

I let out a squeal and scurried away to keep a safe distance. "Heartless woman," I said.

. . .

My father was given a heap of towels before he was ushered back into the black car. The rest of the cast piled into the remaining cars and truck. One final man stood behind the piano, playing a tune as they moved slowly on. The day was warming up and growing brighter as the clouds cleared. My pig coat came off with some difficulty. It seemed to cling to me as I pulled. I folded it neatly as if it were an item of clothing and buried it in the sand by the river.

I wanted to follow my father. I wanted to know what he was like. His party drove along the dirt road that ran parallel to the river. A sudden gust of wind blew leaves off the trees nearby in the direction of my father. In my hand, I carried the four snails I'd picked off the body in the watch house. Each snail, according to *The Book of Explanations*, granted me a costume. I wanted to play the part of a leaf, so that body was granted to me. I was immediately carried away by the wind.

I was one snail less as I landed at the surface of the river, letting the current push me along. The waterway I traveled, having been altered by dams, led me to only one possible destination. Swept ashore where the river ended at a bank, I arrived just in time for the performance in which my father's leading lady played the role that had once been my mother's. She was Nora in a living room scene. She had just arrived home with shopping bags. Her husband appeared at the doorway. She caressed him and showed him her purchases, joining her hands in a sweet plea for forgiveness for getting carried away. The musician tapped out a song on the piano.

I looked for my father and found him sitting in the darkness of the wing space, watching his cast's every move.

In the last scene, Nora walked across the darkened stage with a small suitcase. The curtains came down. The play arrived at its conclusion. My father was the most exuberant in his applause as the masses of people dissipated, leaving by lantern light. My father gathered his cast together, notes scribbled on his hands and arms.

The wind continued to gust across the earth, in the direction of my father. Wanting to be nearer to him without being brushed away, I was one snail less when I decided to play the role of the wind itself, my robes silver and wispy as I bent my body to and fro and blew into my father's stern face. Standing so close to my father, I hoped I played a convincing wind as I scrutinized his features. He had aged, compared to the picture in my mother's jewelry chest. Though other lines have marked his forehead over time, the bird in flight was still prominently at the center. His teeth had a greenish sheen, but he was handsome, with a smooth face and a head of thick and disorganized gray hair. As he went over the performance scene by scene, he pulled his jacket closer to his body.

. . .

I followed my father's entourage until we arrived at a mansion, in which there was an evening party for the actors. In a pristine white dance hall with chandeliers, twelve beautiful young actresses waited for the arrival of the cast. To get closer to my father, I was one snail less when I played the role of the thirteenth beauty. He took the wrist of each young actress and danced with her in a circle around the room. When it was my turn, my father plucked my wrist and brought me onto the dance floor.

"Do you find me attractive?" he asked. I nodded without looking at him directly.

He danced with command, the way he swam, with a grace and fluidity that was unmatched in the room. Except by me, because I was his daughter, though he did not yet know. My skill intrigued him, and when the circle was over he did not part with me. It seemed to the rest of the party that this meant something, as the other actresses began to leave. We circled until the last person in the dance hall left—the leading lady—closing the door of her guestroom behind her.

My father led me to a second guestroom, adjacent to the leading lady's. He swished green tea in his mouth. "How would you like to be cast in my next play?" he asked.

I said, "What will it be?"

"*A Doll's House*," he said.

I groaned. "It is always *A Doll's House* with you. Don't you ever want to do something different?"

"I have perfected it," he said.

"What about *Romeo and Juliet*, *Joan of Arc*, or *Antigone*? I can act a convincing death," I said. I demonstrated on the bed before him.

My father took off his shirt and tried to undo my dress. His entire torso was graying and black in places.

"No," I said. I slapped his hand away. "Not tonight. I'm bleeding."

Though my father looked displeased, he did not push the matter. Instead, he took a handful of barbiturates and fell asleep immediately, holding me in an inescapable grip.

• • •

The next day, the leading lady asked me to tell her of my acting experience. She was cold with me but not unkind. I told her I had none, which made her friendlier with me.

"I came from the National Academy," she said. "Our director selected me from the crowd at a party—not unlike the one last night—a long time ago."

We crouched over the bank of the river as our director took another swim. I bit into a peach and juice dribbled down my exposed leg into the water, raining upon the swirling orange heads of fish.

"Our director's brain is like these wild fish. He is swimming after his mind," she told me. While we waited for his cast to collect him, she detailed to me his unpleasant attributes, as if she'd been waiting to tell someone for a long time but hadn't yet found a confidant. The words charged out of her mouth like bullets: his lecherous eye, bulbous hands against the backs of girls much too young, his poor hygiene, his purple and swollen body from nightly fire cupping procedures, his moodiness in the dark hours when lovers should be intimate. "Now here he is, swimming in a shit-filled river, slowly killing himself. Let him," she said.

"What are you still doing here, with him?" I asked her.

"Every director has his leading lady," she said, "and I am his. There is no place for me outside of this."

My father yelled from far out in the river, treading water, "It is improper to show off, but I can't help it!" He was now being coaxed back to shore, flanked by his actors. My father grabbed the stage manager who could not swim and shook him. "You must learn how to swim," he said with much vigor. "How can you keep up with me otherwise?"

My father was brought a heap of towels to dry off his body. I tried not to look at his infected chest or think about the men back home writhing in their beds. In the black car, I sat by my father. He patted my hand in a fatherly way. We wound around a mountain cliff again and again. My father's leading lady sat in the front and was separated from us by a dark glass. She didn't say a word.

She performed again that night, in a mountain village. I sat with my father in the wing where he ordered for us a spread of fruit and pork. Half the time we watched the play and half the time I fought my father's pull.

He would pull me into him and whisper into my ear, "Watch her carefully. You will emulate her for your debut."

My father's leading lady was a phenomenal actress. She was an entirely different force on the stage—light, airy, mesmerizing. When she was not acting, she was so different. An impenetrable, cold woman, like a fortress. I said this last part aloud to my father.

"She is a good actor," my father said.

I looked back out at the stage. Nora was tired of being treated like a doll. Nora performed the tarantella. Nora silently made a decision.

"What happens to her when I take over?" I asked.

"I will take care of all that," he said. We watched the last scene in silence.

Nora with her suitcase in the darkened doorway. The play ended. My father and I cheered exuberantly.

. . .

Because there was much of my father in me, I was instantly familiar with the stage and with his direction. For a while, I traveled with the cast as the understudy to the leading lady. She never once grew sick, so I remained in the wings watching her, itching to be Nora. It was like this until one night before a performance, I noticed a small slime at the bottom of my satchel that had oozed out of my last remaining snail. I slipped it into her watercress soup while she was not looking. Soon after, her face puffed up and she could not go on.

That was the night of my debut. And from that night onwards, when the leading lady went on stage, the audience asked for me. It was also from then on that the leading lady refused to see anyone, especially me.

. . .

I was warmly welcomed in each village where we stayed on the nights of our performances. At the different mansions where the dances were held, where the twelve beautiful hand-selected actresses from the town came to meet my father, he never met my equal. I was certain he wouldn't. He was vain. He looked for reflections of himself, and I was his daughter though he did not yet know.

Sometimes, I tended to my father as a daughter would. On nights when my father did not look well, I concocted pastes and slathered them across his abdomen and brought him tonics and herbal medicines. Occasionally he would proposition a different intimacy between us, which I would politely decline.

. . .

Those days while I was his star, my father spent hours working on a project in an adjacent guestroom wherever we were staying. When it had grown quite late one night, I knocked at his door.

"What are you working on?" I asked, stepping into the room. There was an earthy and wet odor.

"I'm almost finished," he said.

"What is it?" I asked.

"A severance package," he said.

My father showed me his trunk of severance packages, which was full of terrariums of all shapes and sizes containing the rarest fish and amphibians.

"You collected a pair of exquisite frogs once," I said.

"Yes," he said. He gave me an odd look. "I might have."

. . .

When my father handed a terrarium to his leading lady and sent her away, I was filled with guilt. Yet, I wondered if what I saw was relief on her face when she departed.

After her departure, my father approached me. "You've bled for thirty days!" he exclaimed. "You have not allowed me to do a thing. Yet, you've won my heart and I must have you."

I knew that I could not remain any longer. I felt around in my satchel. I was one snail less when I decided to play the part of the bird, to escape through the window for home, leaving my father yearning for love.

I floated over the earth until I found the frog pond with the two rocks beside it and the watch house nearby. I finally arrived at my body, wrapped in the mantle on the floor of the watch house. I re-entered my body and fell into a deep sleep. When I woke, *The Book of Explanations* had turned into a fine yellow sediment. Our men seemed to have risen from the dead in my absence, as they were outside the window, baring their clean chests as they tended to the chores they'd neglected. I couldn't tell how much time had passed.

. . .

The next time I heard my father's voice was years later. I was at the bend in the Yellow River near the house, carrying my own child in a sling. Our fortunes had turned. The waters were extremely low. There was a big famine throughout the land that wiped out all our crops, and we hardly had enough to eat. We were all becoming dust. He was without his cast, washing his body in a patch of calm silty water. He'd aged significantly since I'd last seen him. I introduced myself to him as his daughter. I told him facts only I would know: My mother's name was Lanhua. She was one of his Noras. He had loved her once and then left her behind with a pair of frogs. He wanted to take a closer look at me. He examined my hair, my ears, my fingers.

"You acted for me," he said.

"I did," I said, "for a short time."

"You were good," he said.

"Thank you," I said. "I only wish you had a more interesting role for me."

I studied my father as he studied me and my baby. He was only a feeble shadow now, his body sitting on his bones like a coat. I could not help but feel sad for him.

"I was trying to clean this," he said, holding the skin of his torso out for me to see. "I've been scrubbing for a long time. But it looks like the black is never going to come out."

I helped him out of the water. A gust of wind blew sand in the direction of our house. We let the next one carry us forward.

NIGHT FLOATS

The sand dunes to the right of my window were moving left very slowly. At irregular intervals the wind picked up outside, scraping more sheets of sand off the dunes and gusting them over the short shrubberies in my direction, flecking the glass pane. A geologic shift was in progress, had been for all time as long as there was wind. It was more noticeable these days because of the weather; it had not rained in months and the air was as dry as a sick throat. I lived in an apartment complex in a city divided by the dunes. During sandstorms like these, it appeared I lived in the dunes themselves, as all the other buildings around me vanished behind a yellow curtain. The sun hovered behind the haze, smeary like it was enclosed in a glass jar.

It was impossible to see the levitators in this terrible weather. I stood by the window listening to the pulse inside of my mouth and wondering what to eat. I had just gone to and returned from the surgeon's, where he removed the wire that had held my jaw shut for the last five weeks. Now my underbite was noticeably gone. I no longer looked like a deep-water fish, but a general pain still remained due to the alterations.

The window was situated in the narrow space between two doors that tended to slap against each other if opened at the same time. But now one door remained shut, as Florence was no longer around. It was the entrance to Florence's personal studio. She was now in an entirely different stratosphere, with the levitators. I used to be one of them. We had gotten quite good at levitation during our time together. At first, we practiced in the house, eating dinner hovering over the table, sleeping directly above the bed, not touching a single piece of furniture for days. From there, we stood by the window and simply stepped into the open air, our bodies rising together, twirling into the higher stratospheres to watch the planes pass and the kite corners dipping in and out of the clouds. During our ascents, we read to each other, tossing a book back and forth and sometimes forgetting it in a tree as we picked wispy branches and braided them into wreaths. As we pushed higher, the air cooled against our skin, and the birdsong died away into a quiet stillness of wings in flight. I remember it was all Florence's touch, her effect on me.

I made myself a shake in the kitchen using a canister of powders that didn't taste like anything, following the doctor's orders of staying on a liquid diet of high calorie protein shakes. Not only did I have jaw surgery but I also had my wisdom teeth extracted in one go. My teeth and jaw, misaligned for some time, had been giving me constant pain and sleep trouble. The procedure was long, puffy, the weeks of recovery like a corridor of mirrors, confounding and repetitive. My jaw had been wired shut, my cheeks numb and bruised. Now, everything in me was aligned, and without the intrusive correction mechanism, I no longer had to inject liquid into the gaps in my mouth with a syringe. I could open it enough to fit a straw and as wide as I wanted as long as I could handle the pain. In fact, along with my shake, I ate a plump marshmallow shredded into small pieces.

As I sipped on my shake, I wandered through the rooms of my house and ended up in Florence's studio. She ran a soap making business in there. I examined a block of soap sitting in a mold waiting to be cut. Because it was an opaque color, I assumed it was made from lye, a caustic chemical not to be touched by bare hands. The soaps that were already cut and complete sat on a shelf wrapped in brown paper. To diffuse an overwhelming presence of fumes, Florence usually measured out the lye on a scale by the window next to a pot of succulents. I remembered the process well: she wore yellow rubber gloves to pour the lye into water, and while waiting for the fumes to disappear, she swirled her protected finger in the canister that contained the white detergent-like substance; she floated over a half-dozen steaming pots, stirred the mixture when it had saponified, added fragrance, and dumped the concoction into molds; she grabbed a knife and cut the large solid formations of soap into smaller pieces. This was how I remembered her: knife in hand, her body hovering over her soap. This was a long process she performed on the weekends, before she took them to the farmer's markets.

As we hovered high up in the air, where we had no boundaries, we dreamed up new lives for ourselves: biking to the Arctic Circle, circumnavigating the world on rollerblades and sailboats, hiking from Alaska to Chile, living remotely in the mountains and backcountry skiing, exploring the last of the wilderness.

Then, I received a promotion at the accounting firm where I worked and gained a barrage of clients. I drooped closer and closer to the furniture until I no longer hovered over my tasks. I looked at them on the ground. I spent all my time on the phone, sitting at my desk and scrutinizing numbers. In those days, Florence often complained that I was statuesque and could not believe how long I could go without moving from my chair. "If you were an ocean dweller, you would by now have been covered by barnacles. And if you were a forest dweller, vines," she often said. She started calling me "Barnaby."

I peeled open the brown paper wrapper of one piece of soap and found little cubes of color sealed within a larger rectangle of glycerin. I unpeeled another, and it was the style that had become Florence's signature: a solid black heart sealed in a transparent pink mold, the sweet and bitter scent of grapefruit. I peeled several more open, and they were all of this make. Was Florence playing a joke on me? All these hearts suspended in glycerin, impossible to reach. It was this batch that she was making before she gave up the hobby. "They won't saponify," she'd said in a gloom the last day she hovered over her pots full of soaps that were not adequately converting from one state to another. She scattered a handful of lye into the air out of frustration. She'd thrown the lye at me so forcefully that it flecked against my face and my glasses and drained into my lap where a searing pain near my penis made me shoot out of my chair. I must have heard her wrong. "*Why won't you saponify?*" she must have been saying to me, realizing that the man slouched over his desk checking numbers was not going to change.

When I was unable to keep up with Florence in our couple's levitations, during the busy seasons at work, she started practicing without me, not only in the daylight but also at night. Thereafter, Florence left the house through the window as I slept and weaved through the fronds at first with difficulty and then with the suppleness of wind. She called these excursions her night floats, drifting just out of my reach. I could see her body through the window as I went over numbers and signed off on work papers, its shape growing small. She came home wearing elegant head wreaths made of branches, leaves, and berries and brought back flowers that she pressed and ripe fruit that she ate. She turned my sleeping body over and spoke excitedly about the brightness of the stars in certain faraway places, a green meteor. Following her return through the window, she'd take a shower to clean off the sand on her body and then she'd sleep restfully. Her night floats grew longer and longer; the more she explored the more she realized she hadn't explored enough. Sometimes I went to sleep before she returned and her side of the bed was still empty in the predawn when I jolted out of a bad bout of bruxism. I was still waiting for her to return the night she took up a new lover and never came back.

I knew this because she'd left a note on the sill, underneath the pot of succulents. She'd fallen in love with a hawk, one with black plumage that shone blue in the light. Now, I wasn't getting good sleep during my recovery because Florence's furniture was vanishing overnight piece by piece and I couldn't understand how. Though I tried to be vigilant, standing by the window and keeping my eyes on the door and the sky, I kept missing the culprit that snuck out her books, jewelry, paintings, and lamps. But now, the big things were disappearing too. Just the other night, Florence's armchair, which I had been using, went missing. Now I had to stand.

I started to wonder if the dog-walker was the culprit. Florence had hired a dog-walker who came around on weekday afternoons to walk her dog, a curly yappy thing. Florence usually left some cash for her on the bookshelf by the door underneath a stone that we'd picked up off of a dark beach. Since Florence had taken her dog when she left, the dog-walker stopped showing up. But I knew that the dog-walker had a set of keys and had never returned them.

. . .

Now that the mouth mechanism was gone, my spirit felt lifted. But, my spirit had for so long been at subterranean levels that now it was merely resurfacing. I drove out to the dunes and went for a stroll through the mounds with my walking stick, letting the wind blow sand wings over me. The wind howled; the air was gauzy. A few boys climbed the dunes with round trashcan lids under their arms, sliding down the steep facades once they'd reached the top. They laughed and laughed. I climbed a great height and considered the undulations below. The wind had stratified the dunes, giving them a combed look. A pair of lovers lay naked at the top of one peak, thinking that nobody could see them. And that was almost true, the wings of sand performing some sort of trick, making them disappear and reappear like an apparition.

I couldn't help but think that I was in a powerful current, my life careening toward a future where I wasn't sure there would be any happiness or fulfillment, a direction impossible to shift away from without a great deal of pain and equal uncertainty.

On my way back, I followed signs for a garage sale and stopped by a condo, where a man on a couch inside his garage waved me over. He sat in the center of a clutter of furniture, various kitchen and bathroom accessories, and a large collection of records and video games.

"Everything is for sale," he said, gesturing at all the items, and then returning to a very thick book. A gray ring of color circled his right eye. His face was fair. He reminded me of a pigeon.

"Are." A dull pain cut through my jaw from lack of use. "... you moving?" I asked.

"No," he said.

"Why are you getting rid of everything?" I mumbled, keeping my jaw in place.

The man contorted his face as he tried to understand me. "It's just things I inherited. There's no room in the house."

"It's all very nice," I said. The furniture was in good condition, antique and expensive looking. I pointed at a mustard-colored chair. It came equipped with gold-plated claw feet. "How much?"

"I don't know. Twenty dollars?"

"That cheap?"

The man shrugged. "It was my rich uncle's. I didn't know him very well. I'm his last living heir, so it was all sent here."

The mustard chair pleased me when I tested it out. I could imagine sitting in it for many hours. "Twenty dollars?" I asked again.

"Yep," he said.

I looked again over all the undervalued furniture and tried to imagine it all in a room: the puffy chairs and ornate tables and chests, the trinkets and wall hangings and rugs. He must not have been a levitator, I thought. He was a man who used his furniture to the fullest. "You'll sell all of this in no time," I said.

The man nodded and then went back to his book. I hoisted the mustard chair onto my back, feeling its heaviness for the first time.

. . .

When I returned to the apartment, I situated my new mustard chair in between the two doors that slapped each other, right beneath the window, and vacuumed up all the sand I had brought in. I stared outside into the hazy environment, and if I squinted a little, I could make out a handful of day levitators. I thought about Florence's light body and wondered how I could possibly learn to replicate its buoyancy without her. Then, I was asleep. I dreamed that I had turned mustard yellow while reading in my chair and then became the chair. Florence, her eyes very black, was so displeased, hovering above me in a black dress. Around her head, she wore a wreath of feathers that gleamed black and blue, plucked from her new lover's body. Then she became the wind and rushed away.

When I woke, I called the dog-walker. I told her that we would have to terminate the use of her services and that I would need her to return the house keys ASAP.

• • •

I only had one memory of the dog-walker. Once, when I decided to work from home while Florence was out of town, I watched the dog-walker arrive right on schedule. I had forgotten to cancel the appointment. When I saw her car pull into our driveway, I put the dog into her crate and hid under the bed. I didn't want to thwart her routine.

The dog-walker came into the house; she removed her sunglasses and set them on the counter; she switched on our record player and sifted around our refrigerator, eating an unnoticeable amount of this and that; she went into Florence's studio, selected a piece of soap, and stashed it in her purse; she turned on the television and put her legs up on the coffee table. Then, she made her way to the bedroom and plopped onto our bed.

I watched her from beneath our bed, below the bedsprings. The bedsprings under her weight pressed gently against my stomach, and while she fell into a brief nap, I continued to check numbers beneath her. The strange sleep schedules of a college student! Eventually, her phone alarm sounded and she dragged herself out of the room to walk the dog.

• • •

"I'm really going to miss sweet Ellis," the dog-walker said when she came by later that day with the key. I thought she had perfectly lovely features, but her mouth was quite large when she smiled. I invited her in. I wanted to ask her about Florence.

"Thank you for your services," I said.

"Yes, of course." She made a gesture with her hand across her forehead and then smiled widely again.

"Have you heard from Florence?" I asked.

She looked at me curiously. "No, should I have?"

"Do you still see Ellis?" I asked.

"No," she said. "I haven't heard from Florence in a while. Is something wrong?"

The dog-walker's eyes darted, fishlike, away from mine in the silence. She scanned the room and must have noticed that Florence's things were gone. There was a long silence. Then she seemed to remember something. She snapped her finger. "May I ask you a question?"

I nodded.

"How can you stand living so close to the dunes?" She explained that she lived on the other side of town, where the problem of the sands was not as extreme. "Where I am, there are way better conditions for levitation."

"I haven't really thought about it," I said. Somehow Florence and I had made it work for a short while. I'd gotten used to the sands and couldn't imagine living without them.

"I'd like to live near water," she added, "like by an ocean or a lake or a pond."

"The ocean has lots of sand," I said.

She shrugged. "Not as much as you have here."

"Florence left me some time ago," I said.

"Yeah, I kind of figured," she said. "Her stuff is gone."

"And you don't know anything about where she is now?" I asked.

The dog-walker shook her head.

I let out a long sigh. I was feeling tired from my trip to the dunes, but I did not want to be rude. I asked, "Would you like some wine, something to eat?"

"Sure," she said, "I wouldn't mind eating a little." I scrounged from the cupboards a half empty bag of marshmallows.

"I'm sorry. This is all I have," I said.

"I haven't eaten marshmallows in a very long time," she said. Her eyes lit up. "Have you ever played chubby bunny?"

After she gave me an explanation of the game, I understood that we were to insert marshmallows into our mouths until absolutely no more could fit.

"What is the point?" I asked.

"It's just a silly game," she said. She inserted a marshmallow into her mouth and took a seat in the mustard chair. I watched her insert another.

I mirrored her and inserted a marshmallow into my mouth, to attempt what my former lover meant by "being light." The dog-walker's face grew grotesque, balloon-like.

"You should see yourself," she said, holding back laughter. "You're going to pop a blood vessel." I followed her into the bathroom where there was a small foggy mirror. I looked at myself in the harsh light and found a face full of discomfort, bulge, and bruises along the jawline from the marshmallows, tooth extractions, and jaw alignment. I turned away quickly and continued, inserting marshmallows into my mouth and aiming them toward my throat so as not to have to stretch my jaw open any further. I began to shake involuntarily. Tears filled my eyes. When I could not see due to a searing white pain, I stopped shoving and forfeited.

The dog-walker screamed while her mouth was still full, "I win, I win," her boots flying into the air as she threw herself back into the mustard chair, which bucked on its two hind legs before she quickly leaned forward to balance out, marshmallows flying out of her mouth.

I sat there silently holding my marshmallows in. This was the worst pain.

"Well," she said. "I should probably go." As she dusted the powder from her pants, I went into Florence's studio, threw a handful of soaps into a brown paper bag, and handed her the bag. She gathered her belongings and disappeared out the doorway, her hand reaching backward, an index finger dangling the ring of keys she'd been using. I took it and shut the door.

I slowly pulled each marshmallow out of my mouth one by one, along with some strings of blood. I realized once the dog-walker vanished that my efforts had been for nothing. She didn't have any information about Florence. I kicked over the mustard chair and went to the restroom to dig out the painkillers.

There was an ugly scar in the hardwood when I returned and pulled the mustard chair upright. The sky outside was dark and despite the haze I could see the lights being turned on in the houses across from mine. When the air was clear, I would sometimes see a dark haired woman in the apartment next door lying naked on her bed with one arm lifted over her head and another stroking her breasts up and down while she watched TV. But on this night, her window remained dark.

I immediately grew tired and foggy-minded due to the pain-killers; the smells of the remaining soaps wafted over to me from Florence's studio, pungent and irritating. I had a dream in which Florence and I each tried to reach the tip of a mountain, I in a car and Florence hovering in the air. The entire time, we traveled parallel to one another, she in the smooth air and I over a bumpy road that rattled my car and brought jolts of discomfort. I woke up in the middle of the night; the bumps had morphed into pulsations in my mouth and head, the work of my heart below made palpable and audible through pain. I took more painkill-ers and, when they took effect, slept fitfully.

I woke again to a rustling and assumed it was a beetle fall-ing out of a vent. But another followed it, and then another. Then there was a thrumming. The sounds came from Florence's studio. I stumbled through the doorway and found a cast of hawks gathered there in an amorphous black mass, populating the sills and the shelves as if in a great tree, piercing their claws through Florence's soaps and through the last of her furniture. I watched their collective silhouette, a bookcase bobbing up and down against their flight.

• • •

The next day was clear day with only a slight breeze. Lifting myself out of bed, I walked into the living room and looked at all the empty spaces that used to be Florence. I did not immediately go to work, though I had scheduled it to be my first day back after my medical leave. Instead, I left the apartment, carrying the mustard chair on my back. The three flights of stairs were troublesome. I entered the teashop on the first floor and placed the mustard chair against the wall where I could look out of a giant window. I ordered something warm. As I waited, I stared at the blue sky, full of levitators interacting with the birds. I thought about Florence. I missed the pleasure of having her body in my periphery, one that would leave but always return to me. As I sat in my chair staring out the window at the calm, smooth sands, the boy who took my order came over and stretched the tea out for me to see, the water forming a long thin cord that then vanished. Florence would be visible in this sky. I watched an ascending hawk waver momentarily in a gust of wind and thought it beautiful in its rise.

HEART SITE

In the island town of Crow, only hearts were planted in the ground to conserve space. Long ago, before I was born, there had been a community meeting to decide which body part should be buried to represent the dead. The decision had been between the heart, lungs, and the brain, with one vote for the eyes. The rest of the body was fed to birds and the bones were burned and mixed into a paste we used to fortify our homes. They became a form of memory.

My mother's heart is buried at the heart site. She was a big woman, loud and direct in love and anger, transparent. After my mother died, I missed her clarity. My father was more masked. I called my efforts to decipher the things he didn't say the Father Algorithm. It required great effort. My mother ran the hot baths for me in the mornings and bundled me up at night to ease my arthritis up until she was too sick to help. I noticed her swollen, purpled extremities as she brought me blankets at night. My mother's was the last shiny, embalmed heart to be buried before the practice stopped in our town. My father and I, our eyebrows raised, witnessed the source of all her ailments being lowered into the ground on the day of her funeral. The attendees ogled at its size. It was the largest and brightest we ever saw. It was truly beautiful.

I visited my mother's heart when I felt up for the walk. The heart site was at the top of a big hill. A woman named Elsinore tended to it. She made her rounds riding in a hand-controlled pink scooter because she didn't have lower legs. She lived in a tiny zome house on the periphery of the heart site and placed strange jelly candies in my hand whenever she saw me, breathing loudly as she asked me questions about my day. I left the jelly for the ants and the disinterested birds at bus stops I passed on the way home.

. . .

For a time after my mother's death, my father stood awkwardly at the entrance to my bedroom at bedtime and asked me if I was keeping up with my studies. My father had an aversion to emotional discomfort and was a perpetual hoverer. I called the unoccupied emotional space around him the Father Bubble. I followed the Father Algorithm to understand that my father felt great love and concern for me. For example: in the cold days after my mother's funeral, my arthritis flare-ups hit me like a dramatic weather change. I woke in the mornings barely able to move my legs. Walking felt like lifting two fat tree trunks. My legs lagged behind the rest of me like a lip-sync error on film. In those days, my father whisked me up and took me to the hospital to get my infusions where we silently watched reruns of swimsuit modeling competitions.

Another example: My father ordered for me a cane that lit up neon green in the dark. I had selected it from a tear-away catalog included in a book called *So Your Child Has Arthritis*. I had told him I wanted to walk to and from school with the others. I was a normal teenage kid, terrified of weakness.

After school, I went straight to the bath to loosen my joints and read comics, the pages lit by the last of the afternoon light streaming in through the blinds. I read until my toes pruned and puckered. While my friends learned how to play sports, I wrote and illustrated my own comics that took place in Crow. My mom, dad, and friends were all characters.

When I finished my stack of comics, I'd suddenly be aware of the silence around me, and a sadness would take over. My room shared a vent with my parents' bathroom. I used to be able to hear them talking, arguing over me, through the vent. It was weird to hear the new quiet.

. . .

In the island town of Crow, to graduate eighth grade, we had to complete a project where we were paired with a civil servant to learn about the benefits of community service. I was paired with Elsinore, the keeper of the heart site, our town expert in historic preservation and horticulture. She was recommended as *someone who understood my condition* and could provide the necessary amenities. We were to spend one week at our assignments and overcome a specific challenge: mushroom picking, bridge repair, or mail delivery, for example.

On the first day of my assignment, Elsinore picked me up from school, and I rode behind her on her scooter. The cemetery grounds were fenced in gold. At the center of the grounds, there stood a large bronze sculpture of an anatomically correct heart. It was a gray day, rainy. My mother's heart was buried in winter. Spring vegetation changed the scenery, making it hard for us to find the sites. Elsinore was quiet, preoccupied. She offered me no jellies. I wondered if my presence was bothering her. The gears in her scooter whirred until she parked it and cut the engine. I couldn't stop staring at that place where her leg ended too soon under her loose flowery skorts.

"Is there something bothering you, Elsinore?" I asked.

She looked at me for a moment, forgetting she wasn't alone. She said, "The hearts are doing something weird beneath us." We tidied up each burial site, removing brambles and dead flowers from the monuments. There were also a number of smaller bronze statues in the area to maintain. We went from statue to statue—each dedicated to the heart—where Elsinore taught me the preservation procedures. As we rinsed and soaped and carefully applied a sacrificial coat of wax onto the greening statues scattered throughout the grounds, she told me about observations that she'd been accumulating over the past few years.

She had noticed, at first, a great increase in the presence of birds of dark plumage in the periphery, feeling as though she was being watched. She had also noted that the entire heart site had expanded in circumference, her scooter route taking up more time than usual. "The earth at the heart site is cracking, and the cracks are growing deeper and more pronounced, disturbing the order. For example," Elsinore said, when we finally arrived at the giant anatomically correct heart at the center of the grounds, "this ginormous thing is leaning dangerously to the left. Careful, don't make it overly shiny."

I eased up with my brush. The detailing was hard work. Every section of the oxidizing sculpture required brushes of varying size. There was an art to the polishing. After we finished with the giant heart, we got back onto the scooter, and Elsinore drove us to a specific burial site to show me more evidence. On the way, she told me about a great exodus of frogs that cleared out from the area all within two nights. In their rush to leave, some had covered the glass windows of her zome house. Elsinore cut the engine. It was dusk, and I was exhausted from a long day's work. I could feel my legs cramping up, and my hands were dry from the rubber gloves. The cicadas were starting to sing.

"Finally," she said, growing excited, her forefinger raised close to my nose, "my scooter wheel got lodged in this, and I almost flipped over my handlebars." She showed me a thick red tube protruding from the soil like an opening to a sewer.

"Is it a piece of an old heart statue?" I asked.

"Well," Elsinore paused. "I think it is a heart, a real one, buried long ago. I'm not sure why, but it has swelled with time." She pointed at the gravestone nearby, the name on it having been worn smooth long ago.

I got onto my belly and peered in. "Don't you want to see inside?" I said.

We studied the opening in silence. It was as if the aorta had just grown out from the heart, breaking the soil, expanding outward toward the sun, like a plant.

"I've tried as recently as yesterday," she said, "but it's dark and winding in there. I've had trouble navigating."

Then, my father arrived at the agreed upon hour to pick me up, and I had to leave Elsinore there hunched over the aorta, her head halfway in.

• • •

Later that week, I woke at 4:30 in the morning when I heard pebbles fleck against my window.

Elsinore was wearing stealth colors—all black—and beckoning to me from atop her scooter. She was unmistakable, her permed black hair billowing behind her in the humidity, her scooter glistening in the moonlight.

"I think the time is now," she scream-whispered into my window. "It's slated to rain soon."

My father was sound asleep, having taken his routine sleeping pills. Walking in the dark, I eased myself with my light-up cane past my father's office, where he prepared tax returns for his clients in Crow. Once outside, I slid onto Elsinore's scooter. She smelled soapy and fragrant and soft, like she had just bathed herself and used a lot of bath salts.

When we arrived at the heart site, the soil shone silver against the sky, the moon huge and close to the earth. I got off the scooter and sat in the dirt to do my morning joint exercises.

"I'll have to leave the scooter behind, so I'll need some assistance," Elsinore explained. She handed me a labeled diagram of a human heart ripped out of her encyclopedia.

I was glad she had chosen me, but I worried. I thought about my classmates, who were starting to develop athletic bodies. Some of them would be capable of lifting Elsinore, of holding her up. She could put her trust in them.

Elsinore was already entering the heart. She pulled herself forward with the strength of her arms as I followed her with my cane into the intersecting arterial and venous corridors of a heart on its side. What started out narrow and claustrophobic when we entered expanded outward into a cavernous space. The sound of the cicadas was thunderous in the underground. I shined my cane into the darkness and admired the interior heart structure that was now hollowed out and empty. How huge it was! Elsinore called out into the darkness, on her elbows, lighting the way with the glow of her cellular phone. When we stopped to rest, we had not reached the center of the heart yet.

We paused for some time. Elsinore handed me a granola bar. We ate in silence. I thought about the ease with which Elsinore navigated the heart terrain without her scooter. I couldn't help asking, "What happened to your legs, Elsinore?"

"It was a birth defect, nothing terribly tragic. Are you disappointed?"

"N-no," I said. "I just don't think you actually need any of my help."

Elsinore said, "Of course not. When I was a child, I was forced into gymnastics classes. I have a cabinet full of pommel horse medals; maybe one day I can show you. I just thought you'd enjoy this."

I nodded fiercely.

"Now where are we?" Elsinore inquired.

I looked at the diagram. "We might be coming across the mitral valve," I suggested, pointing at the structure nearby, which towered like a shark's giant jawbones. It was in a half-open state. The other side was dank and cave-like.

. . .

In the neon-green light of my cane, we saw that the chamber we entered was full of blinking crones. We studied them in their black outfits, some with severe hunchbacks and some without teeth. Some fat and some skinny. Some with such wrinkled faces that all their features were hidden. Some were attractive, like they could still be young. There were crones with spring temperaments and crones of summer and crones of autumn and crones of winter. They stood shoulder to shoulder and on top of each other like circus performers; they were stretching the ventricle taut.

Elsinore and I guided the crones out of the subterranean maze. They chattered behind us. Their cacophony was like the crunchy sound of technology, creating a curtain of turbulence that woke the town in the night. They followed us out of the heart center with matched slowness until we were overtaken. My legs throbbed beneath me, and I was carried out by the sea of crones. When we finally managed to escape the heart, the big moon against the horizon cast strange light, dragging behind it the new day. A crowd had already built up, worked into a panic by the unsteady ground beneath their feet.

With proper count by our town census official and his apprentice eighth grader, the number of crones matched the exact population count of Crow. There was a one-to-one correspondence. We could hear the collective breathing of the crones, clustered together in the periphery. Elsinore led a group of townspeople to the heart center to show them the great mystery. Those who went brought back sketches. They each drew the tear in the heart wall where the crones emerged into our world differently: like a hornet's nest, or like a slit at the back of a skirt, or like a crack in the earth due to drought, or like a great big wound.

. . .

Our initial attempts to communicate with the crones were unsuccessful. It was as if they did not hear us or did not know our language. The crones traveled in giant black balls of appendages that rolled to and fro, knocking passersby off their feet and, on occasion, pitching an unsuspecting pigeon, cat, or lapdog into the wilderness. There was one casualty, involving an elderly woman. We studied their frenetic rolling patterns. Our town mushroom picker and her apprentice eighth grader observed that their movement patterns were similar to the cytoplasmic streaming of slime mold. They snatched things from our town and left it cleaner. They collected the litter from the banks where the land touched the water. We kept tally of all of our possessions that went missing: wristwatches, necklaces, a hat now and then. I called these balls of crones and possessions the Spirals, and numbered them by size.

Spiral 3 frequented my street. My father was revived by this occurrence. They likely traveled in that ball-like form through the vortex into our town, my father observed, the shape having some evolutionary advantages, especially for warmth. "They

are building something," he said, "with the items they take."
My father was the town hobbyist in beekeeping. He studied
his apiary in our backyard and treated his bees with tenderness,
admiring the pollen baskets that accumulated on their hind legs
as if they collected pollen just for him. It was his obsession with
bees that helped us communicate with the crones. After studying their habits for some time, the idea came to him that it was
possible to pry the giant black balls of crones apart, that perhaps
somewhere hidden in the mass, there was a queen.

My father decided that we needed to make a peace offering.
We purchased milk, bread, honey, pomegranates, and hardboiled
eggs. We had Walt at the local grocery store put everything into
a gift basket and tie it with a bright red bow. We left it outside,
sickling the basket handle to a tree. It must have been days since
the crones had eaten, and there was a lot of them to feed. Spiral
3 tumbled in our direction, and for the first time, it skidded to
a halt. A vibration spread through the ball like a cat shaking off
water until a small, hunchbacked crone dressed in white broke
away from the ball to collect the offering. As if on cue, my father
made his entrance upon the scene.

The queen's white garment was soft, almost fleecy like a
sheep's coat, the buttons on it pearly and clean. It contrasted
with the starchy black dresses worn by the crones that were
now standing in a circle around our house waiting for their
next order. The queen's face was small, like I could cup it in my
hands. Her facial features were tucked behind folds of loose skin,
the droops far more varied and more pronounced than the faces
in her cohort.

She studied my father and me and the crowd that was forming around her. My father tried to keep people back, but they
inched closer out of curiosity. Some even took pictures. She
must have been as old as the earth, the layers of flesh around
her face like ancient rock. She grabbed the gift basket. For some

reason I thought about my mother, if she could continue to grow old in some other world outside of this one, where the laws of aging and dying were different, where she learned other ways to move through space. Maybe given time she'd recirculate and return as a crone.

The crone in white slipped back into her ball before my father could talk to her. I heard the news later that all the Spirals in the entire town had frozen in place when this happened, that crone heads peered out in curiosity. For a time, they rolled to and fro in giant ashen balls of heads. Keeping their ears attuned in their daily rolls, they must have learned about us and our language, looking for a way to give back.

. . .

For a few weeks, there were incidents all over town. The Spirals nabbed people as they walked to work, school, or even the grocery store. Our town went into lockdown; we were all warned against stepping foot outside of our homes. But when the first batch of people was returned, they were returned transformed. It was as if they'd stepped into and out of a cold lake, their entire circulatory system reignited. They spoke about their experiences of being taken into a particular lair decorated in their own detritus—strands of hair, fingernails, baby teeth, photographs, credit cards, food wrappers—and then being granted a wish. They each stared into the milky eye of the one crone that chose them as they explained how they wanted to be transformed. They came back as basketball stars, cello prodigies, multilingual speakers, and more beautiful forms of themselves. After that, we all looked forward to the day when the crones would snatch us up. We waited and felt that thrill of anticipation when a Spiral passed us on the street, hoping for our turn. Parents warned their children not to wish for something frivolous. But they could hardly control what we wished for; we were just teenagers. One day a girl in my grade was whisked away and the next day she arrived at school with a pair of perfectly plump breasts. A pimply boy who had been snatched came back with flawless skin.

. . .

The Spirals dwindled in size as each of us returned to our homes. Once a wish was granted, the crone that granted the wish left their spiral and integrated into Crow. They needed something to do. Tasks that a crone could do well were given over to the crones. Some crones could be better than automated services, so the replacement was made. Crones answered phone calls and transferred people between lines. Everybody talked to crones on a daily basis, to pay their bills, their traffic tickets, their loans. Crones repaired electronics. They explained why certain people were not in their offices. Some crones could be better than phones themselves, so we replaced our phones with a chain of crones that whispered our words into each other's ears until they met in the middle.

Some crones could perform the jobs of mannequins. They wore wigs and hats. They stood still on street corners holding signs or in shop windows and modeled all the latest clothes.

Some crones could perform the jobs of certain machines better, so the replacements were made: washing machines, assembly machines, ATMs, voting machines, self-checkout machines, computing machines. The crones learned to provide the services. Some crones could be better than certain equipment, so the replacements were made: farming equipment, medical equipment, sports equipment, amplifiers.

Some crones could tell stories better than books, so they were available at the library. Some crones could be better than games, so we revised rulebooks for games to involve them. Some crones could be better than pillows and beds, so we slept upon a thatch-work of them.

. . .

I don't know what my father wished for when he was gone for a week. Adults usually spent a longer time with the crones. I stayed at my friend Petra's house across the street until he was returned. Petra and I played board games where crones kept score. I stared out the window waiting for a light to turn on in my house. During those long nights, I watched Petra's mother walking through the garden by lamplight silently observing the fruits of her work. Plants grew wild and huge and thrived under her care. Lush produce emerged from the stalks, shiny and bright like gems.

When my father was finally returned, he struck me as having a haggard look, like he'd gone through an operation. I noticed no new skills and no new objects. No new formations on his body that I could see. The change was subtler in adults. He was more talkative with me. He closed down his tax practice to spend time with his bees. We worked on the bees together and started to bond.

My classmates told me that the length of time anybody spent with a crone corresponded with how obtainable these wishes were without the help of a crone. There was a girl in my class that we didn't see for the rest of the school year, or for the rest of my time in Crow. Her dreams must have been big and specific. Maybe she wanted to be able to help a lot of people, or bring somebody back from the dead. Maybe she just didn't want to let go of that feeling that anything was possible.

. . .

I was the very last person in the town of Crow to be granted a wish. For some time, I thought I'd simply been skipped. On the night of my crone visit, my cane emitted its neon-green light as I walked home from the comic book store. My father was going to be late coming home so I had the key ring around my wrist. Having no more crones to form a pattern around her, the queen dressed in white walked up to me as I was unlocking the door.

"Would you like to come in?" I asked. Her fortress of crones had already come down around her. She didn't look like she could snatch me up by herself. She was about as tall as my shoulders.

"Yes, that could work," she said.

When we got in, I asked her if she was hungry. She refused food but asked if we had any milk. When I fetched a glass and handed it to her, she lapped at it with a small gray tongue until it couldn't reach. Then I poured the rest of the milk into a bowl. Thereafter, I fetched bowl after bowl of milk until she was satisfied.

"I didn't think anyone was coming for me," I said.

"Why not?" she said.

"I don't know," I said. "I was just worried."

"Everyone gets something," She took out a yellow matchstick and held it before me. "Tell me, what do you need?"

I gazed into her milky eye. I realized that probably everyone in our town heard these words come out of the mouth of a crone, sitting just the way this one did, like a bundle of compressed, hardened dust that carried magic inside. Facing a crone felt, suddenly, like inevitability, something that everyone had to go through, like puberty.

I was finally going to get something I wanted, something that mattered to me. My heart started to race. How was I going to be changed? My friends had all returned from their crone visits polished and beautiful, athletic and smart. I felt like I was seeing all the people I knew for the first time for all the desires and dreams they each carried; our transformations made us specific. I thought about Elsinore, who now sang as she tended the heart site, her new voice projecting into the clear air a sweetness that I'd never known before.

"I don't know," I said. "I've always wanted a ridiculous superpower, like maybe a hair arm, where my hair could reach far out in any direction, grab something solid, and pull the rest of me with it."

"You want long, thick arm hair?" the crone asked. The yellow match lit up brightly.

"No, no," I said. "That was a joke." The flame went out. "I just want to be arthritis free."

The crone stared at her match, which didn't light. She shook her head at me. "Nature doesn't allow it." She explained to me that she could grant a wish even if there was the faintest hint of a flame. But if there was none at all, I was out of luck.

My spirit was crushed. "My mother back!" I shouted, to test the flame. "Infinite youth!" The match did not light. I cursed at the top of my lungs. The crone put her hand on my shoulder.

"What happens to you after I get my wish?" I asked.

"I dissolve into a light dust," she said. She said it the way someone would say 'I'm going to the store.' "And you will forget about me and continue with your life."

"What about the other crones?"

"The others will be around until the next queen comes. You will forget about them, too."

"If I don't make a wish, then you won't die."

"Then I will follow you for the rest of your days, and there will be a backlog of crones. It will disturb the order if you do not make your wish."

"I don't know what I want," I said, "I'm just a kid."

I thought about a comic book I'd recently read about a

girl who couldn't speak. Her life was very lonely. But then she learned that she could communicate with plants, as a result of all the time she spent alone in the woods. Now that she had this ability, she decided to go on a journey to find the oldest tree in the whole world, to hear its stories.

"When you disintegrate into dust," I said, "I need to remember you." The queen thought for a minute. We both stared at the match until a small flame lit the dark room.

"It is done," she said.

As she chanted her incantations and weaved a ball around me, enclosing me in a pod for some time, I felt a part of me growing old and ancient and wise. As I underwent my transformation, I heard the footsteps of my father, coming in and out of the kitchen, and I could see his figure through the translucent portions of the pod. When I finally emerged, I went straight to my room and huddled in bed. That night, my father visited me there, crossing the Father Boundary and taking me in his arms. "Things are going to change for us," he said. I called that moment the Father Override.

. . .

After the last wish was granted in Crow, a heavy fog settled upon our town. It required us to stay indoors for two days, the visibility levels unsafe for transport. When the fog dissipated, we had forgotten about the crones. They had given us what we wanted and had blended into our environment. People simply ceased to see them. It was like replacing the carpet in the bedroom with hardwood. After some time, we all forgot the carpet had ever been there.

I could still see the crones, long after my friends stopped talking about them, long after my friends forgot how they acquired their best talents and traits. I think my father could see them too, based on how he often gazed out in the distance. What the townspeople didn't know was that the crones had become an organizing force for us. They kept everyone on course and everything orderly. They were responsible for overseeing photosynthesis, seasonal changes, digestion, the school system. Everyone was near a crone, was moving toward a crone. They were atmospheric. They controlled us. Once I understood what they were, I called them the Directions.

I became a writer. I was like a koi fish at the bottom of a clear pond gaping upward at the beautiful patterns of the world, the Directions behind everything. My moments of inspiration were a product of the Directions. The clarity that came and settled upon my mind again and again, I knew, was a gift from them. They are air and atmosphere, wind and rain and canopy and all.

• • •

I wait for the arrival of the next queen crone, returning to the heart site often to see if a new heart is ready. I split jellies with Elsinore. One day, my mother's heart will open, and I will be able to step inside. I often wonder about what I would find there. Titans, Ogres. One day, she too will recirculate.

I know that the Directions maintain a garden in the forest. They get restless from waiting. Every once in a while, teenagers sneak into the patch of land that the crones have claimed, a place where even the animals don't go because of the magic. Their patch of wilderness smells of medicine. The teenagers snatch berries and foliage from the plantings and gorge themselves on them. They speak fluent German, or Thai, or Icelandic. They acquire great skills: computer programming, bookbinding, or knife throwing—but only for a short time. It has also become a destination for people with ailments or broken hearts who need to pass the time.

I go there often. I can still hear the crones' crisp noises as they wander among us in the dark. Sometimes, when I can't sleep, I join their restless pack until I feel better. To the rest of the town, they've adapted their voices to sound something like the animals that activate in the stillness of night.

THE SEA CAPTAIN'S GHOST

Entering the city of Boris from the sea, the Sea Captain's Ghost notices a mollusk on the back of his neck and peels it off. The city is full of flower gardens. People from all over the world come to Boris for its flower gardens, he is told by a billboard. Flower trellis–covered towers jut skyward. When the wind blows, the light catches the falling leaves and petals. A floral scent infuses the salty air. The weary Ghost of the Sea Captain tries to find his way to the Starfish Villa where the Sea Captain's daughter lives, holding a map and asking the men standing outside of their restaurants for directions. They are polite enough to point the way but look at him like he can't be trusted.

There are motes everywhere in this town. He swallows all the motes in view, like little fireflies hovering lazily in the landscape, swept to and fro by the wind. The Sea Captain's Ghost rings the doorbell at the gate to the Starfish Villa. He can see the distinct shape of the house from the gate. The outer shell of the house is a light pink color. There are a total of five arms that convene at the center. Just like a starfish, the roof of the villa has a bumpy pink texture, created by little domed skylight protrusions. There is a weathered plaque on the gate that provides a brief biography of the architect, who designed the villa before walking into the sea. This man is Daphne's late husband. Just like the Sea Captain, the architect was obsessed with the sea. Daphne, wearing a red raincoat, greets the Ghost of the Sea Captain at the gate.

The Ghost of the Sea Captain presents the mollusk to her.

"If it isn't the Sea Captain," she says. She is inspecting his features, how they've changed since he last departed, and something is not quite right. He is more greenish than a regular human. His hair more seaweed than keratin. His eyes like sea glass. His teeth like shells. His beard more seafoam than wiry white. His garments are tattered and sopping wet. Small, barely perceptible waves wash over his form. He is composed of sea matter and spirit matter, his perimeter infirm.

Daphne takes the mollusk from the Ghost of the Sea Captain and holds it in her palm. She's never seen anything like it. The mollusk has a beautiful white translucent shell and is cool to the touch. The patterns on it are like electricity. She wants to hold it against her eyes.

"I am the Ghost of the Sea Captain," he announces.

"How could that be?" she asks. "How did you die?" She makes the gesture to hand back the mollusk, unsure of what it means to accept a gift from a ghost.

The Ghost of the Sea Captain shakes his hands urgently in front of him, splashing Daphne with seawater. "No, no. The Sea Captain is not dead. I am the ghost of the undead Sea Captain. It is all explained in the mollusk," he says.

• • •

The first meeting between the Sea Captain and the Sea Captain's Ghost took place when the Sea Captain saw his own death before his eyes in a tumultuous storm over the Boris Sea, icy waves washing over his body, tipping him toward the infinite waters, the cannons and heavy equipment around him lurching to and fro. He saw the ghost of himself, as the scroll within the mollusk reveals, materializing from sea mist. He thought of Daphne and his grandchildren, losing another fool to the sea.

It was against fate that the Sea Captain survived the storm, losing all his fish and crew. "You were premature," the Sea Captain said to his ghost, when it was just the two of them facing each other adrift on a ruined ship.

The ghost, puzzled to be face-to-face with the man he was supposed to replace, did not know how to retreat to the spirit world now that he'd already been conjured. Because he was premature, he was not as bloodless as a ghost. The coloration of the Sea Captain remained in his features. It was as if the Sea Captain had been twinned. Passing time together, they played chess in the cabin, entrapping each other with the same moves. They prepared sushi from freshly bled fish. They knew each other's hearts.

. . .

Daphne mulls over the scroll for some time before shoving it deep into the mollusk. She realizes that she has two fathers to deal with now, one of them flesh and blood and the other made by the sea. The one that comes from the sea is immune to being swallowed by it, she reasons, and that is like hedging her bets with her impetuous father.

She welcomes the Ghost of the Sea Captain into the villa. They go through one of the narrow arms, where paintings of the Sea Captain, the Rose Scientist, and the Architect hang at crooked angles facing each other. They walk toward the atrium, where a small fountain spews a stream of water at the center of a rose garden. It is the center through which anyone must pass to get to another arm of the villa.

"There is a team of rose makers that live and experiment here," Daphne says. "They invent new roses in the Coral Arm of the Starfish Villa. They can invent the shape, the color, and the scent of the rose. Every rose ever invented lives here."

The story of the rose makers begins where the story of the architect ends, his studio repurposed for a rose lab when he died, in honor of Daphne's late mother, the Rose Scientist. Daphne and the Ghost of the Sea Captain walk through the rose garden. Every flower has a little white label under it. The Sea Captain's olfactory senses are clarified in the Sea Captain's Ghost. The atrium roars with fragrance. The Sea Captain's Ghost looks up and sees the sky and many stars through a clear dome.

"I have memories of being here by the roses," he says, "and looking at these same stars." The memory of the Sea Captain is not clarified in the Ghost of the Sea Captain, as the Sea Captain still possesses it. But yet...

"Whenever the Sea Captain stayed here at the Starfish Villa, he muttered to himself and hermitted in his arm of the house," Daphne says. "I don't know what he did most days."

Then they pass the Mariana Arm, Daphne's room. It is still decorated very much in the same way as when she was a girl. She pauses to put the mollusk into a spare tank. When she turns around, she sees that where the Ghost of the Sea Captain stood there is now only a puddle of slime. Daphne considers mopping away the slime, but she pauses to consider its complexity. The slime consists of marine foliage. She scoops up the slime and puts it all into the tank with the mollusk, giving it an ecosystem. She follows the slime path to the Sea Captain's den—the Serpentine Arm—to find the Ghost of the Sea Captain at rest in the Sea Captain's armchair. His ghostly hands grip the arms tightly the way the Sea Captain's do when he is here. The land is so still in contrast to the sea that it sways just the same. It is in this moment that she truly believes the ghost and the Sea

Captain are one and the same. Small shells are tangled in his hair. Salt crystal lashes. His hairline has receded the way waves pull at the sand and leave it smooth. The smell of something distinctly oceanic strengthens around him as he foams and snores, foams and snores.

. . .

The next day, the Sea Captain's family is piled together on the second floor of a Boris City tour bus. The children complain about the heat as Daphne ties up their hair. Even the boys have long hair. They are exposed to the open air, embarking on a tour of the Boris attractions.

"I have strong memories of Boris," the Ghost of the Sea Captain insists. Steadfast Daphne points out Boris landmarks to him as the wind ripples the Ghost of the Sea Captain's complexion. The Sea Captain's abhorrence for tourism is clarified in the Sea Captain's Ghost.

"It's nice to take the kids out," says Daphne.

The first stop of the City of Boris tour is the Boris Tower. The Boris Tower is the highest structure in the city of Boris, covered in carefully groomed flower trellises and vines. The structure is old and shakes when the wind blows. Paperwork falls out of the windows. The agencies within the tower are divided between The Department of Time and the Department of Space. Historians belong in the Time Department. Eye doctors belong in the Space Department. Investment bankers belong in the Time Department. Yoga instructors belong in the Space Department. The paperwork required to establish a new agency is complicated. Every profession conceivable in the city of Boris is represented with a desk in the Boris Tower of Time and Space. The tour group rides the elevator up to the very top floor and looks out over the town. The Sea Captain's vision is clarified in the Sea Captain's Ghost. The cataracts from a whole life of gazing outward in the direction of the sun and the silver-tipped waves, of squinting into the distance, are gone.

The next stop on the tour is the Boris Museum. The Ghost of the Sea Captain continues to leave a trail of slime wherever he goes. The slime consists of: agar, phytoplankton, kelp, algae, sea moss, sea foam, seaweed, sea glass, sea grass, sea anemones, and coral. Daphne tries her best to swipe away the slime with her feet, but there is inevitable buildup. While they are walking across a smooth marble surface in a hall of sculptures from ancient Boris, an elderly woman from the bus tour slips on a dollop of slime and has to be sent to the hospital. The rest of the tour group gathers around the Sea Captain's Ghost and studies the slime. They pick up ocean pieces and smell them. One daring individual puts a bit of slime in his mouth and swallows.

"I'm a professor of marine botany," he says. "This is all good, edible stuff." The botanist is a very excitable man, and he's made a fantastic discovery. Word quickly spreads of the taste and nutritional content of the slime. The ancient statues are forgotten.

"The slime is multipurpose. It can be eaten. It can be rubbed on the face, like a mask. It can cover the entire body for a hydrating effect. It can be used as shampoo. It can be hardened, shaped into a bullet, and used as a suppository. It can also be used as a poultice," the marine botanist announces.

Daphne remembers being in the Serpentine Arm, standing above the sleeping Ghost of the Sea Captain. The scent of the Ghost of the Sea Captain is lovely. It is musky and sensitive. Surprisingly, it is not a repulsing scent, she thinks. It is not sulfurous like typical ocean smells. People want to draw near it. It is the scent of ghosts. She, too, collects some into her empty thermos. On the other hand, the children are immune to the scent's charm. They stay away from the Sea Captain's Ghost, always making their mother sit in between as a barricade.

· · ·

That night, after the children fall asleep, after the Ghost of the Sea Captain seals himself away in his arm, Daphne reads about ghosts and their specific byproducts. According to the article that she reads, excretions vary depending on the ghost's categorization, whether it is a fire ghost, earth ghost, water ghost, wood ghost, or metal ghost. Water ghosts, the article states, are occasionally associated with life-enhancing goop. Secretions are correlated with their proximity to life-generating sources that emit electrical charges. Ghosts feed on electrical charges in the form of motes, invisible to the human eye. Places of comfort produce fields of motes; thus, their haunting patterns are established.

· · ·

Later the next day, the family takes a small ferry out to the lighthouse island in exchange for a jar of slime. "There's nothing out there anymore," the ferry driver says. "Not for a long time." Daphne is determined to go, so they go. Possessing the runaway heart of the Sea Captain, the Ghost of the Sea Captain enjoys the ride out to sea. The driver of the ferry allows the children to steer. They clamor toward the wheel and argue over who gets to hold it.

"Point the little marker on the steering wheel at the buoy in the ocean. Do you see it?" the Ghost of the Sea Captain whispers between their ears. The boat zigzags across the bay because the kids cannot calculate the ship's swing. They cannot see the buoy because of a gray haze overtaking the sky.

The Ghost of the Sea Captain does not correct their moves. Daphne is surprised that the Sea Captain's foul temper is lost in the Ghost of the Sea Captain. Something has been resolved in the Sea Captain's death, she thinks. The Sea Captain's near death, she corrects herself. The Sea Captain's terrible moods were a byproduct of being alive. She remembers the Sea Captain's gruffness as the terror of her childhood, his fury like the sea itself. It was the great separator.

The Ghost of the Sea Captain sees a great snowy egret perched on a branch of a mangrove. The egret looks like it has a coat on with lace and a fringe around the bottom. The kids gather around him and look where he points. They squeal with glee: "Elegant, simply elegant," they say. Against the wind, locks of their long hair whip in all different directions, like they are dancing.

When they reach the island, they take a footpath from the dock to the ruins of a small amusement park named Pleasure Beach. The sign still hangs, though lopsidedly, at the entryway. The rides were demolished long ago; large heaps of metal and wood are the only evidence of the magic of Pleasure Beach that Daphne remembers. They walk through the ruins. Only the old playhouse is still intact, but it is covered in graffiti and everything within has been looted or destroyed. There is a general smell of mold.

There are squatters living on the island. One man operates a rabbit-roasting machine. In the upper compartment of the machine, a rabbit rotates on a stick. All the juice drips down toward the lower compartment of the machine where roasting potatoes soak in the grease. Another man sells fireworks.

The rabbit roaster says. "People are interested in seeing the ruins. We wanted to be here first, for the early sales."

"People like me," says Daphne.

"Enough time has passed," says his friend, "for this place to be meaningful again."

The rabbit roaster throws another rabbit into the roasting machine. "It's romantic to see ruins," he says. "Everything is tinted by what could have been."

Daphne purchases food for everyone, except for the Ghost of the Sea Captain. He is standing among the ruins, as if he is a part of them. The hazy motes are overwhelming. He used to come here as a boy, he thinks. The memories come together vaguely and then dissipate. The Sea Captain's silence is clarified in the Ghost of the Sea Captain. Daphne is used to the Sea Captain's long silences, the ocean's effect. The children dig their teeth into the rabbit flesh, their mouths shiny with oil.

They are now standing at a sort of cliff, at the edge of the amusement park, overlooking the rocks and the waves. The wind picks up and the Ghost of the Sea Captain considers the treacherousness of the rocks lying just below the surface and peeking out only at low tide. He thinks about the sunken ships, the deaths of sailors, how hard it is to build an afterlife. It is like holding sand in your hands.

· · ·

The Sea Captain's Ghost returns to the Sea Captain, traveling two hundred nautical miles in the blink of an eye. Because he is the Ghost of the Sea Captain, he can return to the Sea Captain anytime. It is a compulsion that leads him back. Upon the ship, there are the waterlogged compartments and there are the dry compartments. This divides the ship into what is the Sea Captain's and what is the Sea Captain's Ghost's.

The Ghost of the Sea Captain wanders through the water-logged rooms of the Sea Captain's vessel and marvels at the objects suspended before him: cases of medicines and salves, bottles of liquor, a ship in a bottle, logbooks open and indecipherable, telescopes, terrestrial and celestial maps, photographs, garments soft and blooming like large white jellyfish, starched uniforms losing their composure, a collection of earthly specimens sealed tightly in petri dishes.

The Ghost of the Sea Captain provides for the Sea Captain. For instance, the Ghost of the Sea Captain gives the Sea Captain fishes by geysering them up to the surface from below. Above water, the Sea Captain can use his pocketknife to make sushi from freshly bled fish and nourish himself back to health. The ghost also provides light, its body giving off an otherworldly luminescence that attracts certain sea creatures to the surface of the water at night.

The Sea Captain's possessions carry some traces that are detected only by ghosts. In the vessel, the white motes are everywhere. The Ghost of the Sea Captain gobbles up every charge in sight. The ship creaks as the waves slam against it. Over the course of several days, the Ghost of the Sea Captain wanders through compartment after compartment of his waterlogged quarters until he's eaten the entire ship clean.

After spending time apart, the two Sea Captains come together to play a game of chess. The Ghost of the Sea Captain tells the Sea Captain about his travels. The Sea Captain nods, but he's only half listening. He concentrates intensely on his moves, like the game is everything. He cannot let the Ghost of the Sea Captain win. And so far, he hasn't. Sitting in command of his ship—blind, feverish, and ailing—he checkmates his ghost.

· · ·

The Ghost of the Sea Captain comes and goes from the Starfish Villa as he pleases. He is the Sea Captain's emissary. When the Ghost of the Sea Captain arrives, he brings a creature from the Boris Sea that Daphne has never seen before. She marvels at the sight of the creature and finds a tank for it. "The Sea Captain is reviving," the Ghost of the Sea Captain announces. "He is on his way back to shore."

After the Ghost of the Sea Captain's departure, Daphne tidies up the Starfish Villa, collecting shells and little mollusks from the rooms. She puts the bigger things into an aquarium, the smaller things into small terrarium jewelry that she wears around her neck or in her ears. She has accumulated many marine creatures now, aquariums and terrariums of varying shapes and sizes full of them, displayed in the various arms of the Starfish Villa. The illuminated tanks cast a bluish light. The rose makers begin to complain because their most recent roses keep coming out blue and smelling of saltwater and sea breeze.

· · ·

The children are sleeping. The Ghost of the Sea Captain and Daphne have dinner at a seafood restaurant. The waiters wear long white aprons that look like dresses. They are tall and handsome and remind Daphne of the praying mantis. Daphne explains to the Ghost of the Sea Captain that the Starfish Villa has no more room for sea creatures. They're getting bigger and bigger. Soon, the Ghost of the Sea Captain will bring her a blue whale. There would be no room for anything else but the ocean in the Starfish Villa. More recently, she has been taking creatures to the aquarium.

"The aquarium has stopped accepting creatures," she says.

"I can't control it," the Ghost of the Sea Captain says. "I am a ghost. I am made of ocean matter."

"I'm starting to feel haunted," Daphne says. She gestures at all of the tiny terrariums she is wearing that clink when she moves. She feels closer to her father than she has for a long time, like they are making up for lost time, but there is once again this great separator. "The Sea Captain is coming back, and when he does you won't have any business bringing me these," she says. She stares at the small light at the end of a cigarette being smoked a few tables down, blinking like a lighthouse.

The Ghost of the Sea Captain considers this fact. He can sense Daphne's unhappiness, but the Sea Captain's most deeply buried desires are clarified in the Sea Captain's Ghost. How does the Ghost of the Sea Captain fit into Daphne's life, into the Starfish Villa when any day now the Sea Captain will return?

When they arrive back at the Starfish Villa, it is near dark and the tanks glow blue in the darkness. Immediately they notice a strange smell. It is a terrible, putrid smell. It crawls up Daphne's nose and shoots a million directions inside her.

Daphne says, "I have to search the tanks."

Daphne opens all the windows to air out the smell. The hanging mini-terrariums clink against each other at the half-opened window, which lets in a small draft. She probes through each tank, searching through the mollusks, the starfish, the monkfish, the seahorses, the jellyfish, sifting for the dead. She handles this swiftly and dexterously, as if this is a regular occurrence. She runs from arm to arm of the Starfish Villa with a scoop, her collection of dead fish growing.

· · ·

The Sea Captain's Ghost thinks of the egret as he makes his way back to the Sea Captain. He is like the egret. The ocean is this great silence over which the egret must pass. It is like the mind, stirring, colliding and crashing against itself. The Sea Captain revels in its chaos, nearly drowns in it, away from the close bearings of people.

Daphne gives the Ghost of the Sea Captain an album of photos every time he departs. He is not in any of the photos though there is always an empty space where he should be. He sits with the Sea Captain as they flip through the photos in the cabin. The Sea Captain gazes at them distantly, his mind secretly churning. Then, the Sea Captain pours himself a glass of whiskey and stares into the face of the Sea Captain's Ghost. The winds roar around the sea vessel. Usually, the Sea Captain's Ghost sits still like the subject of a painting and considers the sunset. This time, he breaks away from the Sea Captain's gaze and begins to set up the chessboard.

SLEEPWATER

When I was a child, I lived in a city within the mountains of China. It was remote and surrounded by natural beauty: pristine lakes, wild horses, and seas of yellow canola flowers. We lived in courtyard dwellings that looked identical from the outside before students from the art school in Kunming came and painted murals of nature on the walls. My mother was an art teacher. It was her idea. In this way, we could say: I live at 'deer' or I live at 'mountain' or I live at 'lake.' Gravel paths snaked between our homes and led us to the city square of government buildings, street vendors selling sweets and trinkets, restaurants with tables in the street, temple grounds, and opera theaters that we crowded into at dusk. Our city was famous for opera. My father was an opera performer renowned for his face changing. He delighted his audiences, who could never figure out his sleight-of-hand techniques.

After one of the last snowstorms of winter, an earthquake destroyed our city. I had just turned nine. My father was at a rehearsal, and my mother was teaching a traditional watercolor class at the middle school while I played outside in newly fallen snow. The entire building collapsed. Part of the school had fallen on me and pinned me down. Some neighbors lifted me from the rubble and handed me to my father. They said, "Take the children to safety. We will look for survivors in the school." My father slung me over his shoulder, led a handful of crying children to the nearest open field, and went back to search for my mother. He was gone for a long time. When he came back, he was alone, his face streaked and dust-covered.

We looked out at our city from the hills, the smoldering rubble of our buildings. The rescue workers came and counted our casualties. I know many people who went mad with grief then, who were changed forever after what they saw.

Some of the elders of our community swore they saw a great dragon break through the earth and chomp at our city before vanishing in a puff of fire and smoke. They declared that they would embark on a pilgrimage into the mountains to find burial sites for the dead. "The qi here is bad," they said. The elders referred to an ancient belief in magic coursing under the earth that could bring prosperity to our dead in the afterlife if they were buried properly. The elders turned to traditional schools of understanding and invited all of us to join.

A small group of us agreed to follow their plans, including my father. We visited the sites of our homes one last time to retrieve all the things that we could salvage: cracked clay jars of mountain vegetables, preserved meats, thousand-year-old eggs. In the rubble of our house, I packed up my favorites among my mother's clothes and pocketed my mother's opera glasses. The glasses were iridescent mother-of-pearl and came with a gold chain. My father didn't take much. He gathered his silk masks, all carefully painted by my mother over the years. That day was the last time I saw my father's true face. For the rest of his life, he covered it with a mask, changing regularly as one would change underwear.

With urns cradled in our arms and our possessions on our backs, we left for the wilderness. I rode on my father's shoulders, my leg in a cast. We followed the river and slept alongside it in encampments. It was terribly cold at night. As we traveled, I peered at the cliffs above us through my mother's opera glasses. I watched wild blue sheep grazing upon the steep cliffs. We moved with the sheep past a landscape of trees covered in tufts of snow, their branches so bare, thin, and plentiful that they were like a layer of fur over the earth.

I passed my father the opera glasses. "Do you see them, the blue sheep?"

My father wore the blue and white mask of a famous soldier from *The Three Kingdoms* with thick brows, a mustache, and a symmetrical flourish at the mouth. He peered through the glasses, through his mask, and tried to adjust their focus. He shook his head and handed them back.

After days of wandering through the wilderness, we came across a snowless landscape, emerald green pools multiplying before us. In them, dark fish pressed their mouths urgently to the edge of the water. A sulfurous scent passed under our noses and led us to a bank foggy with steam, a hot spring that poured over the lips of great rocks. There was an upper level and a lower level of cascading water. We arranged loose rocks to divide the water, creating a pool for each family. This is how our colony beyond the city of ruins was founded. We named it Sleepwater. We lived submerged in water.

. . .

The pool water was thick, almost milky in color at night underneath the full moon, as if it were a blanket that covered my body. Because my leg had to remain out of the water to heal, my head kept slipping, and I'd often startle awake. I studied my father at the opposite end of the pool and tried to copy him. He slept fitfully but his body remained still, his mask like a bodyguard gleaming in the dark, grotesque yet possessing a strange beauty. Masks like those, I was told, had been used in ancient times during war, to intimidate opponents. They were frightening but you couldn't stop looking. My father and I sat in the pool for a long time, like creatures in restless hibernation.

The topmost pools in our colony were scalding to the touch, so we used them for cooking. The water would thicken from the flour residue and grow fragrant because burst dumplings leaked out the scent of oil, chives, fungus, and mountain vegetables. The grandmothers managed the dumpling preparation. They kneaded the dough and rolled it into a skinny tube, twisted pieces off and flattened them into circles, placed a dollop of filling in the center, folded them into tight shapes, and boiled them.

I spent a lot of time with the grandmothers, along with other children who had lost their mothers. The grandmothers taught us how to fold dumplings so that they would not burst. When the grandmothers weren't looking, we drank from the pools and burned our mouths.

In Sleepwater, we found perpetual spring, a patch of greenery. The trees were still leafy, the sky a crisp blue. Time stood still there. The adults labored to develop our colony. They tied ropes between trees and washed our clothing. They tilled the land near the pools. Melon and vegetable seeds were planted. The fastest and most agile learned how to fish. Fruit trees appeared. Everyone was busy. These activities allowed us to stay in the wilderness for as long as we needed. It was easy to put the ruined city out of our minds.

The elders asked my father to perform opera. Every day at dusk, he stood before us in his silk garments and masks on solid ground as we all watched from our pools. During his performances, he didn't play music or sing. I thought of him as a movement artist, somehow able to conjure music and drama with his body alone. Skilled at martial arts, he would hurl his body into the air and land like a cat, his garments flapping around him. His faces told a story, each mask different in color and expression due to exaggerated thickness or thinness of the brows and the eye sockets, varying forehead patterns, and flourishes at the mouth. Our small bobbing audience gave him standing ovations.

. . .

In a few months, I had befriended the other children living in Sleepwater. We tried to catch birds and snakes with our hands. We snuck a gun out of a pensioner's holster while he napped, ran deep into the woods, and shot bullets into the air. When left to ourselves for too long, we quarreled. To occupy us, the elder geomancers recruited us to find burial sites for those that died in the city of ruins. This task required an intricate study of the landforms. We attended lectures where the elder geomancers drew forms into the mud with sticks, and we memorized them as we once did with characters. Certain arrangements of forms sat upon dragon veins, through which the good kind of qi flowed. The elders quizzed us until we understood. Then, every day after we graduated our lessons, we hiked for hours throughout the mountains searching for the landforms that resembled the sketches we memorized. I took my mother's opera glasses and looked through them at the landscape to better study it. The elders drew up a map of the areas we uncovered and marked certain places that looked right. Our excursions exhausted our eyes.

. . .

One night, I woke to the sound of my father leaving the pool and changing into dry clothes. I dressed and followed him into the woods. It was so quiet that I didn't dare make a sound. The ground was wet and cold, but I took off my shoes and followed my father until I could not feel my feet anymore. There was a full moon out, bathing the woods in a faint glow. From my place in the trees, I saw him cross a river and stand before a tree hollow in a clearing. I crept close enough to make out the features on my father's mask, white as the moon.

"Your image is as clear as ever today. I have brought you something to eat. Are you resting well?" He brought with him a plate of dumplings, steaming in his hands, and he fed them one by one into the hollow. He continued to chatter in a familiar way, like how he'd talk at the dinner table, making gestures, his hands forming shapes in the air. Then he was silent for a long time, just staring into the hollow. His shoulders shook. "It's all too much. I'll be back tomorrow," he said.

I had to sneak back to the colony before my father noticed me or found out I was missing. I had this feeling that if my father caught me watching him talk to the tree hollow, it would do great damage to him, like waking a sleepwalker.

While my father slept late the next day, I snuck to that same tree to examine the hollow. "Hello?" I called into the opening. In response, there was an unfriendly hiss of air, the beating of giant wings. Frightened, I ran from the hollow. As I ran, I looked back at the tree and froze. In the daytime, the tree's shape looked exactly like my mother with her back arched and one arm extended as if painting the sky, the hollow where her heart would be. I swore I could see her in every detail. I noticed that the land around the tree looked familiar, too, perfectly resembling a qi formation I had recently memorized: gently sloping mountainsides, a grove of trees, an open space, a river, a gentler breeze. We had found my mother's spirit.

• • •

The children discussed similar findings with each other: a shrub that resembled Mr. Sun, my friend Dong's father; a reflection that appeared in an emerald pool that looked just like Mrs. Wang's daughter, Hua Hua; a rock formation that resembled Jiabi's grandmother. We had discovered our dead living among us as forms in nature.

On our next geomancy hike, we stayed close to the elders.

"What happens if we find exactly what we've been looking for?" we asked.

"That would be propitious," they said. "What did you see that makes you so certain?"

"A sign," we said. The kids looked at each other knowingly. "What happens next?"

"So near to the pure magic of an immense energy flow, our dead will flourish in the afterlife and bless our families from the supernatural world. The great emperors of our country were endowed by ancestors whose tombs were placed just right."

"How did they know where to place the tombs?" we asked.

"That's hard to answer," they said, "If you are so fortunate, the universe guides you to a site. You need to search with much effort, but the thing you are looking for may never be found. If you are lucky, it finds you. Make sense?"

We shook our heads. "Not really," we said and winked at each other.

The elders looked at each other. "We'd like to see what you discovered."

I put my mother's opera glasses to my face to study the mountainsides. I focused on the wild blue sheep huddled together descending vertical cliff faces from where they spent the winter, mothers leading their newborns. I watched the smallest one make its way down to water, struggling on its tenuous legs, looking around anxiously before finally slipping its tongue out to take its first drink. For a moment, it seemed that all the blue sheep looked at me.

· · ·

On my tenth birthday, I went to the hollow and walked around my mother ten times, touching the bark and running my finger through the leaves of her branches. I wore her dress, had knotted it at the side of my leg so that it would fit. I sat down next to her and made conversation. "I want to go back to the city," I said, "the way it once was. I want to go back to school and play with my friends. I want to paint masks with you. I want to learn father's secrets. I don't want to live in Sleepwater anymore." I started to cry. I caught a faint whiff of my mother's floral face cream on the dress. "But I know you're here now, mom," I said, "and I won't leave you here alone." I looked up into the hollow and found a face, white and spectral, looking down at me. It was an owl spreading its great wings to hunt. Its plumage was bark colored, decorated in compressed patterns that revealed them- selves like paper fans when it burst out of my mother's heart. The sun started to set, casting an opaque light upon the woods. Through my mother's opera glasses, I followed the owl on its hunting course. By the time it returned to the hollow, the sky was dark. I lifted the glasses off my face and felt a deep circular crease around each of my eyes.

As long as I continued to visit my mother's spirit, I watched the owl that lived inside her as if it were her emissary. I saw it take flight and return in silence, departing and returning at dusk and dawn, its white face in the darkness like a ghost in the sky. It emitted a low-pitched hoot, a sound I memorized.

· · ·

I noticed that in the year that we lived in Sleepwater, my father developed a cough that rattled his chest. He would save strength for his performances and then lie still in our pool gazing at the sky through his mask. He hardly slept or ate. I worried for his health.

"Father, we have to return to the city," I said.

He shook his head. "It's too soon to return," he said.

"It's been a year," I said. "You need to see a doctor," I said.

My father shrugged. He was stubborn and often neglected himself. It drove my mother crazy.

"I know where you go," I said to him.

"What do you mean?" he said.

"You go to that tree," I said.

My father was silent for some time and then started to nod imperceptibly.

"Well, what do you see there?" my father said.

"I see Mother's spirit," I said. "Why did you never tell me?"

"I cannot point to a tree and tell you it is your mother," he said. "You'd think I was crazy. I'm relieved you found her for yourself."

"There is an owl that lives in Mother's heart," I said. "I feel a great love for it."

My father nodded. "She is here with us," he said. "Visit her often."

"Father," I said, "there are others."

•   •   •

That afternoon, instead of the usual opera show, my father and I gathered everyone together, and we visited all the dead we could find. We showed the elders the landmarks of the dead—all the trees, shrubs, rocks, and puddles that resembled the people that we could once hold and touch. We stood before the dead and bowed, moving from spirit to spirit until it was too dark to see. "Thank you for helping us see them," I said to the elders.

. . .

We stopped going on geomancy hikes, and we began to live as if we'd always lived in Sleepwater. I turned eleven years old, and my father let me have my own pool. I started to hold hands with a boy named Hang who lived two pools down from me. We'd frequently wander through the forest together. He was the only one in his family to survive. We visited his family members and talked to them, slept under their shade, cooled our faces in their faces. Then we visited my mother. We found comfort in Sleepwater, a space that housed the living and the dead. But one night when I was sleeping in my pool, there was a low, vibrating sound that stirred me awake in a panic. The earth was shaking.

From my place in the pool, I saw a large herd of wild blue sheep coming into our colony. Their horns stood thick and heavy on their heads. They formed a circle around us. Some of the sheep had focused on the urns we kept in various hiding places. They dug up dirt with their hooves, nudged at the urns with their noses, and sniffed at them. They stomped to get our attention.

I jumped out of the pool and ran toward my mother's urn. The blue sheep surrounding it froze and looked at me. I picked it up and protected it. Then the sheep looked out into the woods. They moved tentatively toward the forest from which they came, glancing back at me every once in a while, as if checking to see if I would follow. I stood there in my underwear shivering and dripping water as the last blue sheep disappeared into the darkness. I realized after they were gone that only I was awake to witness them come and go.

. . .

When my father woke up the next morning, he coughed up bright green phlegm.

"Dad, I think it's time we buried Mom's ashes," I said. "I don't think we can wait any longer." I thought about the urgent look in the blue sheep's eyes as they nudged at the urns.

I spoke with the elders, who agreed. We could not further delay the rituals. Two years had passed, and we had to face our ruins. Once a handful of us started to bury our urns, other families followed. Each family went to the landform where the specter of their dead resided and performed the burial rites.

My father and I brought my mother's urn to the tree. We temporarily set my mother's urn in the hollow as we dug a hole at the base of the tree. We dug for a very long time. When we tried to retrieve the urn, it wouldn't budge. It had bonded with the tree.

We burned paper money as an offering. My father wept behind his Monkey King mask, from *Journey to the West*. It was my favorite story as a little child. As I knelt and bowed to my mother before the flame, I felt the earth hot and pulsing under my hands.

Soon after we completed the burial ritual at the tree, I noticed that my mother's opera glasses stopped working. The lenses were milky when I looked through them, like the pools of Sleepwater. I never saw anything through them again.

The next day, when my father and I returned to check on the urn, my mother's tree was gone. I was convinced this meant that she finally made safe passage into the realm of the dead, but I could not help but feel a deep sadness that there was nothing of her left on Earth. She was now free of form and swimming in powerful qi.

"Send me some magic so I can come visit you," I said to the space where she used to be.

. . .

The harvest moon holiday was coming up. We would celebrate this one last event together as a colony in Sleepwater and then return to the city. The grandmothers were hard at work folding dumplings for the entire colony. I spent the afternoon helping them. I told them about the owl who once lived in my mother's heart that no longer had a home. They listened and noted that something had fallen from the sky near our colony recently.

"It was like a shooting star, a bright white color," the grandmothers said.

"Where?" I asked.

They pointed toward the east, the direction of my mother's tree.

I scoured the woods near the hollow with Hang for several days and finally found something brown and white dangling from a tree branch. It was an owl mask. When I held it up to my face, it fit perfectly. I wrapped it in my shirt and took it back to Sleepwater.

That night was the harvest moon. The moon was so bright that we could see each other well into the night, and everyone stayed up later than usual. We ate moon cake and drank rice wine heartily. We would pack up our colony and head back to the city the next day.

As soon as my father was fast asleep, I left the colony to find my mother's burial site with the owl mask tucked in my shirt next to my heart.

"Thank you," I said. I left behind a moon cake.

· · ·

That night, the blue sheep came for me. Needles fell from the sky and entered my skin until I was covered in a layer of soft fur. When I stood upright, I was one of them. I knew that our journey over the mountains would be a long one. I ascended with them to the narrow mountaintops where no humans have ever been, the sky so open and bright. All along the way, I could read the bark of the trees. They were like messages to us from the dead, a mixture of the old language I had learned in school and the markings of birds and worms. It would only be a short distance now to the heavens, they read. At the rooftop of the Earth, I looked up. There was still a vast expanse to cross. I remembered the owl mask I carried and knew how to go the rest of the way.

THE SPIRIT MUSEUM

When the ferry came to a halt at the shoreline of the island and let out a great bellow in the night, the passengers aboard stirred from their sleep and started to look alive. Nergüi joined the others as they disembarked and shuffled toward land. She paused to let her eyes adjust as the crowd moved beyond her. The path at the end of the pier split in multiple directions toward an assortment of inns and bed and breakfasts for the visitors. This was where they would scatter for now, but they would all likely see each other again at the Spirit Museum.

Nergüi found herself walking alone on a quiet road. Carrying a weekend's worth of clothes and a heavy case of tools, she followed the street signs to the inn she'd selected on the internet. On the way, she noticed an ease that seemed almost curated in the island features: doors left wide open, bikes splayed on lawns, deer prancing through yards unafraid, a name painted neatly above the entryway to each house, like *The Promise Kept.*

When she arrived at her inn, she noticed that the sign above the doorway was written in a barely-legible doctor's scrawl, the letters squished to one side. *The Pink Palace,* she inferred. She rang the doorbell and a voice from inside said, "It's open." The entryway was cluttered with empty frames, dusty furniture, and antiques. Broken mirrors, shattered porcelain figurines, and big plastic mares dismantled from a carousel leaned against the walls. She sneezed from the dust.

Nergüi waved at the innkeeper, who greeted her from the kitchen. He introduced himself as Sven. He had long silvery hair and the iciest blue eyes. He wore an old captain's jacket with the sleeves rolled up. He gestured for her to sit across from him at the kitchen table, upon which sat a small coffee cake, and cut her a slice.

Nergüi took a bite of the piece of coffee cake. She hadn't had anything to eat at all since the morning. "Pardon the mess. This place used to be an old general store and I'm slowly turning it into a bed and breakfast," Sven said. "Truthfully, it will probably be a work in progress forever."

"The cake is really good," she said. Sven nudged the coffee cake toward her. She helped herself to another slice.

"Are you here for the Spirit Museum?" he asked.

"Yes," she said.

"Well, lucky you," he said.

She nodded. Tickets to the Spirit Museum were sold to the public by a lottery system. Names for admittance were drawn a month in advance. Some people waited years to get in.

"I'm looking forward to it," she said, "but I also have a lot of work to get done this weekend. Is my room quiet?"

"I think you'll like it," Sven said. "What are you working on?"

"A miniature. I make portable replicas of things," she told him.

When Sven gave her a puzzled look, she rummaged through her backpack and pulled out a miniature of the world's largest ball of twine, an exact replica of the original that fit in her palm.

Sven was delighted, throwing his hands up in the air. "The world's largest ball of twine has turned into the world's smallest ball of twine! How is it done?"

Nergui explained how her measurement tool collected spatial data and then transferred it into a modeling program on her computer that she then scaled down to a very tiny size and printed with a 3D printer.

"All the paint and final touches are done by hand," she said.

It was late, past midnight. Sven took her empty plate and placed it upon a heap of dirty dishes next to the sink. "Let me show you to your room," he said.

· · ·

In her guestroom at the top floor of the inn, Nergüi tried to sleep but a sound persisted through the night: a foghorn blowing at regular intervals over the water followed by a higher pitched response, warning ships in the night of the boundary between water and land. They were like the pings emitted by her spatial measurement device as it collected perimeter data. The pings were like an indication of solidity.

Back when he was alive, Nergüi's father received a steady stream of work orders that took the two of them all over the world. He made miniatures for the movies, for tourism bureaus, for government agencies to mark up in color-coded pushpins, and for the few collectors who wanted a replica of the Paris monuments or the Yellow River to walk through in their yards. Nergüi designed miniatures as her father's apprentice until he died suddenly one night of a heart attack in a hospital room by the sea in Split.

"When I die, I want to be fed to the birds," he once said, but Nergüi buried him next to her mother in the Mongolian steppes.

Nergüi in her native language meant "nothing" or "nobody." After her mother died, she was given that name so that bad spirits would spare her, as if she was granted a cosmic invisibility.

There were girls with beautiful names in her hometown, derived from flowers and natural phenomena and other things of value. But there were always a handful of nobodies in her classes, a name that marked the owner of it with a distant loss or tragedy.

Her father moved the family to America, so that he could work in show business. He designed sets for films before he became an independent miniaturist and traveled all over the world. When Nergüi felt homesick from all the traveling, he built for her a miniature of their hometown in the Mongolian grasslands, complete with its tiny yurts, temples, camels, and horses.

"When you are conflicted inside, just look at this. It will bring you peace," he said.

She liked the perspective she had of the town, as if she were a god. Just as Buddhists prayed through beads, she would finger each feature of the landscape and say prayers into the night until she fell asleep.

. . .

The next morning, Nergüi woke up in a bubblegum pink room, a detail she hadn't noticed in the dark. All was quiet. It was strangely comforting, like she had been swallowed and now lived in the belly of a giant being. She walked over to the desk in her room, which was positioned right below a window. The sun slipped brightly into the room. From there, Nergüi could see the strange island features—fruit trees in the foreground, cone-shaped volcanoes covered in snow in the distance, a rosy sky. Because her appointment at the Spirit Museum was not until later in the afternoon, she opened her suitcase and emptied it out.

Nergüi searched for the ring box that carried the miniature of her mother. When she was young, Nergüi had asked her father to build it. He hesitated and did not build her for a long time. When he did so, the replica of her mother was so small she fit into a clear pill capsule that Nergüi kept tucked in a ring box. Nergüi used tweezers to pull the pill capsule out of the slit and set it down on the desk. Then she plugged in her father's microscope and turned it on. The materials he used to make her mother were kept in clear partitioned petri dishes. Inside the compartments were dust, lint, hair, pieces of fingernails, and paintbrushes fashioned out of sewing pins and lashes and diamond dust.

Using the same materials, she started to work on a half-finished version of her father to match the one he had done of her mother, as a tribute to him. She'd completed the lower body some months ago and had finally arrived at the neck. Using a microscope, she competed with her own heart and memory, sculpting between heartbeats to finish his face. It felt like a foolish effort. Her hand had always been imprecise. She lacked the discipline and rigor her father had. She was more of a free spirit. Her mind always bent toward fantasy, forgetting the actual details of faces and things. She had no photographs.

Sven sent up tea on a dumbwaiter. Nergüi heard the wooden spool over which the rope ran shaking in its place as the tea made its way to her, spilling half its contents. Later in the day, he sent her an overripe banana. She worked until she exhausted her eyes.

· · ·

When it was time to leave for the Spirit Museum, she gathered up her father's measurement device and the tickets she'd purchased in advance and left the inn.

The Spirit Museum was the next place on her father's list, though she couldn't tell based on reading his notes if the scheduled trip to the Spirit Museum was for a client or for fun.

Among a list of sites he needed to visit for work, he always inserted a few places that he called "treats." Lately, Nergüi had been losing her father's customers like crazy. Yet she couldn't stop looking at her father's planner. So here she was. This place seemed different than the others. Before boarding the ferry, she'd read a number of articles that guessed at why the spirits of wild animals liked to gather there, what weather features made this island a place of contact between the earthly and spiritual realms. Nobody knew for sure, but people came from all over the world to see.

The entrance of the Spirit Museum was a solid arcing barricade painted expertly to blend in with the wilderness around it. It extended higher than the tallest trees and as wide as she could see in the periphery. From the air, it would have looked like a bright green open parenthesis followed by a sprawling wood. There were places where the green paint was cracking and peeling. A woman collected tickets and handed out pamphlets from a little window in the barricade. She instructed Nergüi that every visitor must be escorted through the Center by a spirit animal and that she was to wait for her own on the other side. Nergüi went through a skinny door that swiveled people in and out like a dark room entrance.

On the inside, the tall walls of the waiting room were glittery white like alabaster. Alongside it, sculptures and busts of animals were evenly spaced, their bases buried in flowers and gifts. A stony trail went into the woods in a loop. Narrow paths veered away from the loop toward various amphitheaters.

Nergüi's father used to take her out on training excursions. They practiced taking measurements of the most difficult landscapes. Like an ice palace, where waterfalls had frozen in place in jutting angular formations of icicles and crystals, or like the complex ceilings of glowworm caves. This might have been one of those trips, she thought, as she turned on the measurement device so that it could collect landscape data. How would she measure something that was entirely spiritual?

The measurement device stopped pinging, having captured the general shape of the barricade and amphitheaters. As Nergüi packed up the tool and waited around for her spirit guide, she watched people enter and exit cubes. Nearby, she heard shouts of exhilaration, of fear, of surprise. There was laughter, weeping. To pass the time, she read through the pamphlet to understand the place.

Soon, a little dog wearing a cone wandered up to her. Her name was written on a little kerchief around his neck in an ornate blue cursive. She wanted to reach out and touch it but remembered what she had just read in the pamphlet: do not touch your spirit guide. The dog, a terrier, started making its way to the nearest amphitheater, but with its head in a cone, it padded over nervously and kept pausing to see if she was following. They entered together. In the darkness of the swiveling door, her name on the dog's kerchief glowed.

Each amphitheater she entered held something attractive. In one amphitheater, an immense collection of tapestries woven with golden threads hung in the air. These golden threads formed lush wilderness patterns. A machine moved the tapestries left and right at intervals of time so that they looked like a bushy tail swishing to and fro. The movement was what attracted the spirits of wildcats Nergüi only ever saw in nature documentaries. They were sleek, iridescent, and milky.

It was their feeding time.

"What do they eat?" someone asked a woman wearing a Spirit Museum jumpsuit.

"Salt," she said. She threw buckets full of salt at the spirits.

In another amphitheater, an antique walk-through flight cage painted a gold color contained a botanical garden with flora from all over the earth to attract flying spirits. Offerings rested inside nesting boxes. The flight cage was packed full of spirits flitting from offering to offering, pecking at the large salt crystals left for them, dyed in a rainbow of colors. Nergüi could hear the thrum of their wings beating, the tiniest of birds to a condor.

In another amphitheater, an entire rainforest environment had been stimulated by zoetropes, magic lanterns, and holograms. Each device set up in the amphitheater grounds contributed to the layers of the rainforest, and the entire environment sparkled and flashed. Shapes were projected to beckon to the creatures of the rainforest. Spirit monkeys studied projections of bananas dancing in a tree.

In a newly constructed amphitheater at the edge of the Center, there were gorgeously designed doghouses, catbeds, and tanks as well as elaborate machines whirring at all hours that chucked tennis balls or knit mice high up into the heavens to lure the spirit cats and dogs down. Nergüi's guide wagged his tail most intensely as they toured that cube. People gathered inside with photos of their pet dogs, cats, hamsters, or fish.

In each amphitheater, Nergüi set the measurement device on the ground and turned it on. The pings captured the décor in each amphitheater but passed through all the spirit animals. She had to rely on her own memory and notes to record them. She sketched their shapes. *Use a combination of dragonfly and white moth wings for their textures*, she wrote.

When a voice announced over the loudspeaker that the Center would close in thirty minutes, one enclosure remained. It was smaller and elevated above all the others. Nergüi and her guide padded toward an elevator. They arrived at a hard bone-white platform in midair. The platform was higher than the walls of the Center, out over the trees, and hidden in a bowl of dark-colored clouds. She could see the spectacle of all the other amphitheaters below.

With closer inspection, Nergüi realized that the bowl of dark clouds surrounding the platform was a shimmering curtain of ashy fish packed closely together, schooling and shoaling. It was the veil between the worlds, she had read in the pamphlet. She watched spirits cross through the veil to the other side. Because it was the closing hour, spirit animals were now leaving the world in large icy masses. But as Nergüi was watching them whoosh past her and depart, she noticed a lone elk arrive from the beyond. They stared at each other. Then a pair of human hands reached out of the coat of elk hide and peeled off a mask, revealing a girl's face.

"Hello," Nergüi said. "Who are you?"

The elk coat the girl wore had tiny asymmetrical buttons all the way down the front that looked like baby teeth. She laughed. "The spirits that visit you are sometimes not those of the animals," she said.

"Why are you here?" Nergüi asked.

"There is nothing quite like this earth," she said. "I just want to remember it."

Nergüi said, "My father died recently. Do you know him?"

She said, "I'm sorry, I don't know him. But maybe you can give me a message to send to him if I meet him someday."

"Tell him I miss him," Nergüi said. "Tell him I am okay, and continuing his art, though I am losing his customers like crazy."

The girl closed her eyes and nodded. When she opened her eyes again, she took Nergüi's hand. "Warm," the girl said. The girl didn't feel as cold as Nergüi expected.

"Is there a message you'd like to pass on through me?" Nergüi asked.

The girl thought for a moment. "I don't think I know any people down here anymore."

They walked around the platform and looked over the edge toward the Center laid out in a panoramic view below. The girl's elk coat flapped in the wind. Below, the spirits ascended looking vaporous and rosy from the sunset. The girl, too, was turning a rosy color. "I must go down," she said. "I have to be quick." She buttoned up her coat, put her elk mask back on, and descended.

The light was changing, and the spirit animals were starting to vanish. A voice announced it was the Center's closing hour. As Nergüi and her spirit guide descended back to the earth, she witnessed the sunset colors rising, the sweep upward of everything below until the Center was deserted but for the ordinary people.

"Salt overhead," she heard a man shout. Gusts and gusts of multicolored salt wafted through the open air. A woman next to Nergüi tilted her head back and opened her mouth. She stood there for some time, letting the salt fleck against her face.

. . .

Nergüi returned to the Pink Palace, where Sven was hosting a potluck. Everyone was wearing a nametag indicating how long they'd been on the island. Nergüi walked around with a giant question mark on hers. They milled about the ruins Sven had been collecting.

Later that night, Sven told her that all the objects collecting dust in his house had at some point in time been used for one amphitheater in the Spirit Museum that attempted to attract humans. Sven hauled the unsuccessful load of objects home for storage because people never came back for them. "It never worked," he said. "Perhaps human spirits were afraid their visitations would do more harm than good."

Nergüi thought about this. "Maybe they are visiting us disguised as animals." She kept the elk-girl to herself. It was possible that she had imagined her completely.

"Maybe," he said. "There's a nice thought."

After the party, Nergüi went back to her room in the Pink Palace and returned to work. She thought about her last days with her father, how neither of them had ever expressed their love for the other in any direct way. His sudden departure left a gaping emptiness inside her. How could she measure something that was entirely spiritual, she thought.

She finally finished her father's face, giving him the head of an elk. It was on her mind. She tucked him into a capsule and set him next to the miniature of her mother. She put the capsules in her mouth and swished them around for a while. Then, she turned on the measurement device and turned off the lights. In the darkness, it shot out a series of points that rotated in space. Nergüi connected the points on her computer to form the physical structure of the Spirit Museum. Everything within was empty, devoid of any creature or pattern. While staring at the emptiness, trying to recall everything that was uncapturable, she thought of the big open landscape in the steppes, where the land was flat with unmarked roads and people lived miles apart. To communicate, they shouted from the outside of their yurts the name of the person they were trying to reach, and—when they received a response—relayed their message into the sky. Mongolians had voices that carried. In an environment of hardly any vegetation, a voice could travel forever.

THE CAVE SOLUTION

Because I felt an empty space in my chest that would not go away for a long time, I filled it with nature. I volunteered for a procedure allowing me to grow a tree inside my body. I went to a greenhouse outside of the city to get the seedling implanted inside of me. It means that I do not have very long to live now, but maybe the tree will carry on some part of my spirit. It's better this way. I want to experience what it is like to have life inside of me, but I don't want to have children. The human race is overpopulating the earth.

Because a tree is growing inside of me, I feel the emptiness fade to make room. I wonder if this is what pregnant women feel carrying babies in their wombs. I've known many women to become pregnant and deliver as I've been incubating my tree, which takes several years—a slower process inside of a human body. My sister is having her fourth child. She's sent me a photograph of herself wearing a "THIS IS MY LAST ONE, SERIOUSLY" shirt with a little decorative arrow pointing at her belly. She is beaming, and a healthy glow radiates from her skin. I think she is a good mother. She should have all the world's unwanted children.

I rent a cave along the side of a cliff overlooking the Pacific Ocean where stalagmites and stalactites are inching toward each other over time. It is better for the tree, which is in its last stage of growth inside my body. My rent is discounted because I volunteer in the wilderness preserve where my cave is located. I install wood posts and string wire through them for park visitors. I put caps on the posts along the cliff trail so that their tips don't splinter when it rains. I count birds in the early dawn and deer at night. Sometimes, I help with the removal of invasive species of plants.

When it is my time, I will make a pilgrimage away from the ocean and into the old-growth forest where the type of tree I am incubating thrives. I was told that my pathway would be innate, that I would just know when and where to go, so I trust my tree and don't worry about preparations. It all reminds me of the behavior of animals who migrate immense distances to mate and reproduce. There's something ancient inside of them that brings each generation back to the same places.

There are others who rent caves nearby. It's a perfect place for simple living and extreme concentration. My neighbor's name is Varun. He has dark hair and it flows down his back. He is a drummer. I think he must be the best drummer in the world, if only for the devotion he has to his art and finding the perfect acoustics. He is especially skilled at the ghatam, a clay pot with a narrow mouth. It sounds good in caves. It is a cave inside a cave. I am mesmerized by his hands as he slaps it, fluttery and fast like butterflies.

Astrid lives in the cave above me, the only one that gets direct light. Her hair is dyed a silvery blue. She makes tapestries out of glass beads. Her cave is the most splendid of all. Its mouth, which faces the sun, is like a stained glass cathedral window. I can tell that Astrid contains great sadness, but it emerges in the world as beauty and light. She works on a very long tapestry as she stares out at the quiet gray air and the great waves crashing against the cliffs. I've asked her about her project. She will be done when the tapestry finally touches the sea.

And finally, there is Leopold, who is the youngest of us and wears his flaming red hair in a bowl cut. He collects mushrooms, often disappearing into the woods to go hunting after it rains. He brings back a small cardboard box full of the strangest shaped fungi. It's heaven out here for mycophiles.

Sometimes we get together around a fire and talk about our lives. Every once in a while, we pause everything we do to listen to the rumble of wild elk as they cross overhead.

. . .

I read a lot at night: erotica, romance, sex books with lots of pictures. I am not interested in relationships anymore but in the feelings that pictures and fantasies elicit in me when I am alone. I want the tree to remember the parts of me that hurt and pulse around it, what it's like to long, to be sensual, to be self-sabotaging for experience.

I open a book called *Transcendental Sex* when I cannot sleep. I skim through it and look at line drawings of nude couples in positions of closeness. Each page prescribes an exercise. My favorites are the Love Mantra and the Heart Mantra. The Love Mantra goes like this: when you take a breath, you imagine that you are filling your body with love. When you breathe out, you say "love" and imagine that you are sending all of your love out into the world. The result is that by the end of the practice, you should be loudly chanting "love, love, love." I have woken up my neighbors doing this. The Heart Mantra goes like this: I place one hand over my heart and the other I rest on my genitals, and through breathing exercises, I travel the pathway between them, the center point being the tree.

I can feel the tree growing inside of me in the quiet, participating in these exercises. It's a pulsating thing when I lie still. I can sense it striving. When I burp or fart in my cave, I get a whiff of the earth that is building up inside of me. I am on a meatless diet of strictly what I can find nearby: mushrooms, plants, herbs, and berries. My scat starts to look like that of a wild animal.

. . .

There are some things that we cave dwellers have in common. For instance, we love the wilderness. We are sensitive. Holidays make us feel melancholy. We are claustrophobic and nervous in crowds. We could go full days without opening our mouths. Out here, we live sparsely and celebrate one holiday: the brightest full moon night that illuminates the forest in this particularly beautiful way. On this night, we celebrate clarity and openness.

In preparation for this day, we make puppets in shapes of nature, effigies constructed out of forest brush. They are big and elaborate. Mine is a fish; Astrid's is a bright bird; Varun's is a bat. Leopold builds a fantastical creature that he sees in his dreams. We march through the forest with our puppets. The deeper we go, the bigger and taller the trees. We pass large spruces, an abundance of skunk cabbage.

Leopold leads us to the dwelling place of the Humongous Fungus. On the surface, it doesn't look like much: a white stripe on some trees here and there, slowly cutting off their nutrient pathways. But the Humongous Fungus bubbles up from under the earth, where it is colossal, one of the largest organisms in the world. We offer up our puppets for it to devour. We contemplate its destructive power, the shortness of life. Silently, I ask it to spare the tree growing inside of me. Varun plays his hand drum, and we dance ecstatically until we fall asleep in the woods.

・ ・ ・

Leopold invites me into his cave after our visit to the Humongous Fungus because he wants to show me something. He lights his lantern and leads me toward a dark, damp corner of his cave. We bend down and our faces touch. He points at fungus growing on two sides of his cave. On one side, the fungus is a yellowish orange color, and on the other side it is a dark green. "If you watch fungus grow toward each other, you can determine if they are both part of one individual. When they meet, they will either blend into one or release toxins and try to kill the other."

"Nature is cutthroat," I say. We watch for a very long time, but the fungus doesn't grow before our eyes. Leopold strokes my arm, but I pull it away. "I'm sorry," I say. "I can't decide what to do with the time I have left."

・ ・ ・

The tree inside of me is taking over. I leave my cave often and sit at the edge of a cliff staring at the sun, my arms extended. I root my feet into the sand. Astrid joins me with her beadwork in hand, threading her tapestry as she chats with me. "You're brave," she says, "for giving up your life."

"I hope the tree carries something of me when I go," I say. "I have been trying to imbue it with human depths, but lately I've been thinking that maybe the tree growing inside me is causing this depth that I didn't feel before. I can't tell."

I watch Astrid meticulously bead her tapestry and think that we are not so different. We both want to leave behind something beautiful, something that connects us to colossal time, like the land and sea.

・ ・ ・

When I was at the greenhouse, I was told that I would fight back; I would struggle with letting go when the time came. At night, I can't sleep, and even the mantras don't help. My ears burn. I am full of regrets. It is then that I begin to hear the voice. It's a quiet, slippery voice that speaks in pulses and streaming cytoplasm instead of words.

I follow the voice down through the cave system, further in than I've ever gone before, crawling through a maze of holes and tunnels until I am underground. I shine my flashlight in the direction of the voice. Then I see its source: a glowing, yellow, bulbous system of fungi. It oozes down in strands before me. The Humongous Fungus is calling to me in the darkness. My tree translates.

"Great forests die," the Fungus says, "but I have lived and thrived for thousands of years. What are you?"

"I am human," I say. "Our lives are short, but we try to live them with purpose. What are you?"

"I am the passage of time," it says. "I wanted to meet you, and your tree."

I protectively cover my belly with my hands. "What will happen to my tree?"

"Don't be afraid. It will grow big and tall and soak in many days of sun and rain. We shall live entwined in the forest for a long time before I devour it," it says.

"I will go where you can't find it," I say, "far from here."

"Dear human," it says, "but I am the voice that you've been waiting for, the one that will lead you home."

• • •

After my encounter with the Humongous Fungus, I return to Leopold's cave and I lie down next to him on his green blanket.

"You're shivering," he says.

"I don't want to be alone," I say. We take off our clothes and press our bodies together. Though I can recall a lifetime of feeling out of place in human skin, I am touched by how perfectly our bodies fit folded into each other. A mound of soil pours out of me.

The next morning, as Leopold sleeps, I look for the fungi growing in the corner of his cave. When he wakes up, I report to him that they have blended peacefully into one.

· · ·

There is a party for me in advance of my departure. We eat sautéed mushrooms and drink honey-wine. Varun plays the ghatam at my request, and I watch the flutter of his hands one last time. Astrid gives me a little patch of blue green beadwork to place beside my tree, to remember the ocean by. Her tapestry is so close to touching the ocean that she hesitates to finish. "It's my life's work," she says. "I don't know what's after." Leopold is quiet, pensive. They all promise that they will stay with me, walk with me into the forest, and visit my tree.

When I actually do hear the soft voice of the Humongous Fungus calling for me, I sneak away and leave the others behind. All along the path, the trees have been taken over, and this image unsettles me. The odds seem against my tree, but I know it is time for me to make room and go. The woods are covered in this mossy carpeting. It is so soft. When the Humongous Fungus tells me I've arrived, I kneel upon the ground and gasp out a puff of dust and look up at the sky. I breathe into my tree one last time, and then I am gone.

ACKNOWLEDGMENTS

"Acting Lessons" describes a few scenes from *A Doll's House* by Henrik Ibsen. The lines recited by the narrator—"Hasn't a daughter the right to protect her dying father from worry and anxiety? Hasn't a wife the right to save her husband's life?"—are spoken by Nora in Act I.

"The Cave Solution" refers to some meditative exercises described in *Transcendental Sex: A Meditative Approach to Increasing Sensual Pleasure* by Jerry Gillies.

Thank you to the editors at the literary magazines that gave homes to these stories. Earlier versions appeared in the following publications: "Bloom" in *The Tusculum Review*; "Soft Breast Mechanism" in *Birkensnake*; "Skin Suit" in *Quarterly West*; "Something Close" in *Tarpaulin Sky*; "Cazenave" in *elimae*; "Acting Lessons" in *Interfictions*; "Night Floats" in *Bat City Review*; "Heart Site" in *The Collagist*; "The Sea Captain's Ghost" in *Heavy Feather Review*; "Sleepwater" as "The Owl in My Mother's Heart" in *Denver Quarterly;* "The Spirit Museum" in *LIT*; and "The Cave Solution" in *Black Sun Lit*.

Thank you to Lily Hoang, Noah Eli Gordon, and everyone at Subito Press for making this book possible; to HR Hegnauer for the cover and book design; to my writing teachers at Washington University in St. Louis and at Brown University; to Jay Brown at the Lijiang Artist Residency for extending his courtyard home to me for a writing summer way back when, where some of these stories first began as observational notes; to Allie Werner for reading through an early draft of this collection; to Pat Hadley for the careful proofreading; to my family and friends for all that you do and help me see, and to Emerson for so many good things.

SUBITO PRESS TITLES

2008

Little Red Riding Hood Missed the Bus by Kristin Abraham
With One's Own Eyes: Sherwood Anderson's Realities
    by Sherwood Anderson
    Edited and with an Introduction by Welford D. Taylor
Dear Professor, Do You Live in a Vacuum? by Nin Andrews
My Untimely Death by Adam Peterson

2009

Self-Titled Debut by Andrew Farkas
F-Stein by L.J. Moore

2010

Moon Is Cotton & She Laugh All Night by Tracy Debrincat
Song & Glass by Stan Mir
Bartleby, the Sportscaster by Ted Pelton

2011

Man Years by Sandra Doller
The Body, The Rooms by Andy Frazee
Death-in-a-Box by Alta Ifland

2012

We Have With Us Your Sky by Melanie Hubbard
Vs. Death Noises by Marcus Pactor
The Explosions by Mathias Svalina

2013

Because I Am the Sea I Want to Be the Shore by Renée Ashley
Domestic Disturbances by Peter Grandbois
The Cucumber King of Kėdainiai by Wendell Mayo

2014

As We Know by Amaranth Borsuk & Andy Finch
Liner Notes by James Brubaker
Letters & Buildings by Thomas Hummel

2016

Sometimes We Walk With Our Nails Out by Sarah Bartlett
Someone Took They Tongues. by Douglas Kearney
New Animals by Nick Francis Potter
To Think of Her Writing Awash in Light by Linda Russo

2017

Dear Enemy, by Jessica Alexander
Camera by Maxine Chernoff
A Forest Almost by Liz Countryman
Sam's Teeth by Patrick Culliton
He Always Still Tastes Like Dynamite by Trevor Dodge
Genevieves by Henry Hoke
Confessional Sci-fi: A Primer by Kirsten Kaschock
Anti-Face by Michael Nicoloff

2018

Your Love Alone is Not Enough by Richard Froude
Our Colony Beyond the City of Ruins: Stories by Janalyn Guo
When the Bird Is Not a Human by HR Hegnauer
ever really hear it by Soham Patel

ABOUT SUBITO PRESS

Subito Press is a non-profit literary publisher based in the Creative Writing Program of the Department of English at the University of Colorado at Boulder. Subito Press encourages and supports work that challenges already-accepted literary modes and devices.